Love Comes Softly

Books by Janette Oke

*Another Homecoming**
Celebrating the Inner Beauty of Woman
Janette Oke's Reflections on the Christmas Story
The Matchmakers
Nana's Gift
The Red Geranium
*Return to Harmony**
Spunky's Camping Adventure
Spunky's Circus Adventure
Spunky's First Christmas
*Tomorrow's Dream**

CANADIAN WEST

When Calls the Heart   *When Breaks the Dawn*
When Comes the Spring   *When Hope Springs New*

LOVE COMES SOFTLY

Love Comes Softly   *Love's Unending Legacy*
Love's Enduring Promise   *Love's Unfolding Dream*
Love's Long Journey   *Love Takes Wing*
Love's Abiding Joy   *Love Finds a Home*

A PRAIRIE LEGACY

The Tender Years   *A Searching Heart*

SEASONS OF THE HEART

Once Upon a Summer   *Winter Is Not Forever*
The Winds of Autumn   *Spring's Gentle Promise*

WOMEN OF THE WEST

The Calling of Emily Evans   *A Bride for Donnigan*
Julia's Last Hope   *Heart of the Wilderness*
Roses for Mama   *Too Long a Stranger*
A Woman Named Damaris   *The Bluebird and the Sparrow*
They Called Her Mrs. Doc   *A Gown of Spanish Lace*
The Measure of a Heart   *Drums of Change*

DEVOTIONALS

The Father Who Calls   *Father of My Heart*
The Father of Love   *Faithful Father*

———

Janette Oke: A Heart for the Prairie
Biography of Janette Oke by Laurel Oke Logan

*with T. Davis Bunn   99A

Love Comes Softly

JANETTE OKE

BETHANY HOUSE PUBLISHERS
MINNEAPOLIS, MINNESOTA 55438

Published by Bethany House Publishers
A Ministry of Bethany Fellowship International
11400 Hampshire Avenue South
Minneapolis, Minnesota 55438
www.bethanyhouse.com

Printed in the United States of America by
Bethany Press International, Minneapolis, Minnesota 55438

ISBN 0-7394-0474-1

Dedication

To my dear friend and former teacher,
Mrs. Irene Lindberg.

JANETTE OKE was born in Champion, Alberta, during the depression years, to a Canadian prairie farmer and his wife. She is a graduate of Mountain View Bible College in Didsbury, Alberta, where she met her husband, Edward. They were married in May of 1957, and went on to pastor churches in Indiana as well as Calgary and Edmonton, Canada.

The Okes have three sons and one daughter and are enjoying the addition to the family of grandchildren. Edward and Janette have both been active in their local church, serving in various capacities as Sunday-school teachers and board members. They make their home in Didsbury, Alberta.

Preface

The life of the pioneer holds much appeal for present-day Americans—and well it should, for it is to these strong, courageous people that we owe so much of our heritage. The question still comes to us: Why do we who have so much take such pleasure in reliving the past with those who had so little? The answer, perhaps, is not too obscure. When the "little" that one possesses comes so grudgingly, there is careful sorting of priorities. If life is simple, the simple things held onto must be of lasting value. Life tends to lose its clutter and only what is of true worth is accepted and cherished—be it material possessions, friends, personal attitudes or spiritual concepts.

Because of my interest in the past and my respect for our forefathers, I chose as the setting for my novel, the period of the pioneers.

For many months I lived, in my imagination, with Clark and Marty and the other members of my book until they shaped into definite characters in my mind—characters that would remain constant when put down on paper.

I feel that they have much to share with us. Clark had a deep trust in His Heavenly Father; even in adverse times he was constant and caring. Though unpolished, he was a true gentleman.

Marty, though young and spirited, had a genuineness, an openness, and a determination that kept her holding on when life was difficult.

I have shared my thoughts with you in the hope that you will feel inspired to reach out to the all-knowing God of Clark and Marty, and that you will catch a glimpse of what human love was truly meant to be. Tender, compassionate, and yes, gentle, that's what *Love Comes Softly* was intended to be. I hope that you will find it so.

Table of Contents

1. The Grim Reaper 11
2. A Mama for Missie 18
3. Marriage of Convenience 23
4. Morning Encounter 29
5. Iffen I Can Jest Stick It Out 37
6. Housecleanin' 42
7. A Welcome Visitor 49
8. It's a Cruel World 55
9. The Lord's Day 63
10. Neighborly Hog Killin' 70
11. Togetherness 73
12. Finishin' My Sewin' 76
13. Ellen 82
14. Missie 87
15. Disclosed Secret 96
16. Thoughtful and Carin' 99
17. Mysterious Absence 103
18. Christmas Preparations 107
19. Snowbound 111
20. A Visit from Ma Graham 122
21. A New Baby 130
22. Ma Bares Her Heart 134
23. Visitors 138
24. New Discoveries 148
25. Fire! 151
26. Barn Raisin' 158

27. Laura 161
28. The Big Day 164
29. Planting 169
30. Sorrow 175
31. New Strength to Go On 178
32. Love Comes Softly 181

Chapter 1

The Grim Reaper

The morning sun shone brightly on the canvas of the covered wagon, promising an unseasonably warm day for mid-October. Marty fought for wakefulness, coming back slowly from a troubled and fitful sleep. Why did she feel so heavy and ill at ease—she who usually awoke with a bounce and a readiness for each new day's adventure? Then, as it all flooded over her, she fell back in a heap upon the blankets from which she had just emerged and let the sobs shake her slight body.

Clem was gone. The strong, boastful, boyish Clem who had so quickly and easily made her love him. Less than two short years ago she had seen him for the first time, self-assured, almost to the point of swaggering. Then in only fourteen months time she was a married woman, out West, beginning a new and challenging adventure with the man she loved—until yesterday.

Yesterday her whole world had crumbled about her. The men who came told her that her Clem was dead. Killed outright. His horse had fallen. They'd had to destroy the horse. Did she want to come with them?

No, she'd stay.

Would she like his Missus to come over?

No, she'd be fine.

They'd care for the body. His Missus was right good at that. The neighbors would arrange for the buryin'. Lucky the parson was paying his visit through the area. Was to have moved on today but they were sure that he'd stay over. Sure she didn't want to come with them?

No, she'd be all right.

Hated to leave her alone.

She needed to be alone.

They'd see her on the morrow. Not to worry. They'd care for everything.

Thank ya—

And they had gone, taking her Clem with them, wrapped in one of her few blankets and tied on the back of the horse that the neighbor should have been riding but who was now led slowly, careful of its burden.

And now was the morrow and the sun was shining. Why was the sun shining? Didn't nature know that today should be as lifeless as she felt, with a cold wind blowing like the chill that gripped her heart?

"Oh, Clem! Clem!" she cried. "What am I gonna do now?"

The fact that she was way out West in the fall of the year, with no way back home, no one here that she knew and expecting Clem's baby besides, should have worried her. But for the moment the only thing that her mind could settle on and her heart understand was the pain of her great loss.

Clem had come out West with such wild excitement.

"We'll find everythin' we want there in thet new country. The land's there fer the takin'."

"What 'bout the wild animals—an' the Injuns?" she had stammered.

He had laughed at her silliness and picked her up in his strong arms and whirled her round in the air.

"What 'bout a house? It'll be most winter when we git there."

"The neighbors will help us build one. I've heered all 'bout it. They all help one another out there."

And they would have. They'd have left their much needed crops standing in the fields, if need be, while they gave of their time to put a roof over a needy, if somewhat arrogant and reckless, newcomer, because they knew far better than he the fierceness of the winter winds.

"We'll make out jest fine. Don't ya worry ya none," Clem had promised.

They had stopped at a farmhouse in the area and Clem had made inquiries. Over a friendly cup of coffee the would-be, new neighbor had informed him that he owned the land down to the creek but the land beyond that, reaching up into the hills, had not yet been claimed. With an effort, Clem had restrained himself from whooping. The very thought of being so near his dream filled him with wild anticipation. They hurried on, traveling a bit too fast for the much-mended wagon. They were so near their destination when a wheel gave way, and this time it was beyond repair.

They had camped for the night, still on the neighbor's land, and Clem had piled rocks and timbers under the broken wagon in an effort to keep it somewhat level. In the morning they had found that more bad luck was theirs, for one of the horses had deserted them during the night. His broken rope dangled from the tree to which he had been tied. Clem had gone, riding the remaining horse, to look for help, and now he wouldn't be coming back. There would be no land claimed in his name, nor a house built that would stand proud of its ownership.

A noise outside attracted her attention and she peeped timidly from the wagon. Neighbors were there—four men with grim faces, silently and soberly digging beneath the largest spruce tree. As she realized what their digging meant, a fresh torment tore at her soul. Clem's grave. It was really true. This horrible nightmare was really true. Clem was gone. She was without him. He was to be buried on borrowed land.

"Oh, Clem. What'll I do?"

She sobbed until she had no more tears. The digging continued. She could hear the scraping of the shovels, and each thrust seemed to lay bare her heart. Time stretched on.

Suddenly more sounds reached her and she realized that other neighbors were arriving. She must pull herself together. Clem would be ashamed of her.

She climbed from the blankets, tried to tidy her unruly hair and quickly dressed in her dark blue cotton frock. It seemed to be the most suitable thing she had for the occasion.

Grabbing a towel and her comb, she slipped out of the wagon and down to the spring to wash away her tears and straighten her tangled hair. This done she squared her shoulders, lifted her chin and went back to meet her new neighbors.

There was a kindness in all of them. She could feel it. It was not a piteous thing, but an understanding. This was the West. Things were hard out here. Most likely every neighbor there had had a similar time, but you didn't go under—you mustn't; you must go on. There was no time nor energy for pity here—not for self, not for one another. It took your whole being to face what must be faced. Death, too, must be accepted as part of life, and though it was hard, one carried on.

The visiting preacher spoke the words of commitment. He also spoke to the sorrowing, who in this case consisted of one lone, small person, the widow of the deceased; for one could hardly count the baby that she was carrying as one of the mourners, even if it was Clem's.

The preacher spoke words that were fitting for the occasion—words of comfort and words of encouragement. The neighbors listened in silent sympathy to words similar to those that they had heard before. When the brief ceremony was over, Marty turned from the grave toward the wagon, and the four men with the shovels turned to the task of covering the stout wooden box that had kept some of the neighbor men up for most of the night to have it ready for this day. As Marty walked away, a woman stepped forward and placed her hand on the slim shoulder.

"I'm Wanda Marshall," she said. "I'm sorry that we don't have any more than one room, but you'd be welcome to share it for a few days until you sort things out."

"Much obliged." Marty spoke in almost a whisper. "But I wouldn't wanta impose 'pon ya. Sides I think I'll jest stay on here fer awhile. I need me time to think."

"I understand." And the woman moved on.

Marty continued toward the wagon and was stopped again, this time by an older woman's gentle hand.

"This ain't an easy time fer ya, I know. I buried my first

husband many years ago an' I know the feelin'." She paused a minute and then went on. "I don't 'spose you've had ya time to plan." Seeing the slight shake of Marty's head she continued.

"I can't offer ya a place to stay; we're full up at our place. But I can offer ya somethin' to eat, and iffen you'd like to move yer wagon to our yard, we'd be happy to help ya pack yer things, and my Ben, Ben Graham, will be more'n glad to help ya git to town whenever yer ready to go."

"Thank ya," Marty murmured, "but I think I'll stay me on here fer awhile."

How could she say that she had no money to stay in town, not even for one night, and no hope of getting any? What kind of a job could a young untrained woman in her condition hope to get? What kind of a future was there for her anyway?

Her heavy feet carried her on to the wagon and her weighted hand lifted the canvas flap. She just wanted to crawl away, out of sight, and let the world cave in upon her.

It was hot in there in midday and the rush of torrid air sent her already dizzy head to spinning. She crawled back out through the entry and flopped down on the grass on the shady side of the wagon, propping herself up against the broken wheel. Her senses seemed to be playing tricks on her. She swam through unrealism into an intense feeling of loss. Round and round in her head it swept, making her wonder what truly was real and what imagined. She sat mentally groping for some sense to it all, when suddenly a male voice made her jump with its closeness.

"Ma'am."

She looked up—way up. A man stood before her, cap in hand, fingering it determinedly as he cleared his throat. She recognized him vaguely as one of the shovel bearers. He evidenced tall strength, and there was an oldness about his eyes that his youthful features declared a lie. Her eyes looked to him, but her lips refused to answer his address.

He seemed to draw courage from somewhere deep inside himself and spoke again.

"Ma'am, I know thet this be untimely—ya jest havin' buried yer husband an' all—but I'm afraid the matter can't wait none fer a proper-like time an' place."

He cleared his throat again and glanced up from the hat in his hands.

"My name be Clark Davis," he hurried on, "an' it peers to me thet you an' me be in need of one another."

At the sharp intake of breath on Marty's part, he raised a hand and hurried on.

"Now hold on a minute," he told her almost as a command. "It jest be a matter of common sense. Ya lost yer man, an' are here alone." He cast a glance at the broken wagon wheel.

"I reckon ya got no money to go to yer folks, iffen ya have folks to go back to. An' even if thet could be, ain't no wagon train fer the East will go through here 'til next spring. Me, now, I got me a need, too."

He stopped there and his eyes dropped. It was a minute before he raised them and was able to go on.

"I have a little 'un, not much more'n a mite—an' she be needin' a mama. Now as I see it, if we marries, you an' me—" he looked directly at her then, squatting down to put himself more on her level, "we could solve both of those problems. I would have waited but the preacher is only here fer today an' won't be back through agin 'til next April or May, so's it has to be today."

He must have seen the look of sheer horror in Marty's eyes.

"I know. I know," he stammered. "It don't seem likely, but what else be there?"

What else indeed? thought Marty's fuzzy brain. I'd die first that's all. I'd rather die than marry you—or any man. Get out. Go away. But he didn't read her raging thoughts, and went on.

"I've been strugglin' along tryin' to be pa an' ma both fer Missie, an' not a doin' much of a job of it either with tryin' to work the land an' all. I've got me a good piece of land an' a cabin thet's right comfortable like, even if it be small, an' I could offer ya all the things thet a woman be a needin' in exchange fer ya takin' on my Missie. I be sure thet ya could learn to love her. She be a right pert little thing." He paused. "But she do be a needin' a woman's hand, my Missie. That's all I be askin' ya, Ma'am. Jest to be Missie's mama. Nothin' more. You an' Missie can share the bedroom. I'll take me the lean-to. An'," he hesitated, "I'll promise ya this, too. When the next wagon train goes through headin' east where ya can catch ya a stagecoach, iffen ya ain't happy here, I'll see to yer fare back home—on one condition: thet ya take my Missie along with ya. It jest don't be fair to the little mite not to have a mama."

He rose suddenly.

"I'll leave ya to be a thinkin' on it, Ma'am. We don't have much time."

He turned and strode away. The sag of his shoulders told her how much the words had cost him. Still, she thought angrily, what kind of a man could propose marriage to a woman who had just turned from her husband's grave—even this kind of a marriage? She felt despair well within her. I'd rather die, she told herself. I'd rather die. But what of Clem's baby? She didn't want death for him, for her sake or for Clem's. Frustration reigned within her. What a position to be in. No one, nothing, out in this God-forsaken west country. Family and friends were out of reach and she was completely alone. She knew that he was right. She needed him and she hated him for it.

"I hate this country! I hate it! I hate him, the cold miserable man! I hate him! I hate him!" But even as she stormed against him, she knew that she had no out.

She wiped her tears and got up from the shady grass. She wouldn't wait for him to come back in his lordly fashion for her decision, she thought stubbornly, and she went into the wagon and began to pack the few things that she called hers.

Chapter 2

A Mama for Missie

They rode in silence in his wagon. The preacher was at the Grahams where he had gone for dinner. Missie was there too, having been left with the Graham family for the older girls to look after while her pa was at the funeral. They'd have the preacher speak the words, pick up Missie and then go on to the homestead. Marty sat stiff and mute beside him as the wagon jostled on. She lifted a half-dead hand to push breeze-tossed hair back from her hot face. He looked at her with concern in his eyes.

"Won't be too long now. It's powerful hot in the sun. Ya be a needin' a bonnet to shade yer head."

She sat silent, looking straight ahead. What did he care about the hot sun on her head? What did she care? Nothing worse could possibly happen to her. She turned her head so that he couldn't see the tears forming against her will. She wanted no sympathy from this heartless man beside her.

The horses trudged on. Her body ached from the bouncing of the wagon over the track of ruts that was loosely referred to as the road.

She was relieved to see the homestead of the Grahams appear at the base of a cluster of small hills. They drove into the yard, and he leaped lightly down and turned to help her. She was too numb to refuse, fearing that if she tried it on her own she'd fall flat into the dust. He lifted her down easily and steadied her on her feet before he let her go. He flipped a rein around the hitching post and motioned her to precede him into the house.

She noticed nothing of her surroundings. Her mind refused to record anything in its befuddled state. She remembered only that the door was opened by a surprised Mrs. Graham who looked from the one to the other. She was aware that others were there, apparently waiting for the call to the mid-day meal. In the corner she saw the preacher in conversation with a man, who, she supposed, was Ben. Children seemed to be all around. She didn't even try to discern how many. Clark Davis was talking to Mrs. Graham, including the preacher and Ben in his explanation.

"We has decided—"

"We—" she stormed within herself. "Ya mean you."

"We has decided to marry up while the preacher be still here to do the honors. It will mean a home fer Missus Claridge here an' a mama fer my Missie."

She heard Mrs. Graham's, "It's the only sensible thing to be a doin'," and the preacher's, "Yes, yes, of course."

There was a general stir about her as a spot was cleared and in what seemed almost an immoral shortness of time she was hearing the familiar words. She must have uttered her own responses at the proper times, for the preacher's words came through the haze . . . "now pronounce you man and wife."

There was a stirring about her again. Mrs. Graham was setting extra places at the table and encouraging them to "set up an' eat with us afore ya go on." And then they were at the table, the children having been fed by the older girls before the grown-ups arrived home from the funeral. The preacher blessed the food and general talk continued on around her. She must have eaten something, though she later could not remember what it was nor if it had been tasty or otherwise. She felt like a mechanical thing, moving, even speaking automatically—with the controls handled by something quite outside of herself.

They were moving again. Getting up from the table, making preparations to be on their way. The preacher was tucking away a lunch that had been prepared for him and saying his farewells. One of the older Graham boys led his horse up from the barn. Before the preacher left the house he turned to Marty and in a simple, straightforward manner took her hands in his and wished God to be very near her in the coming months. Ben and Clark followed him to his waiting horse, and Mrs. Graham said her good-bye from the open door. Then he was gone. Mrs. Graham turned back into the room, and the men went toward the hitching rail to get Clark's team ready to move on.

"Sally Anne, ya go an' git young Missie up from her nap an' ready to go. Laura, you an' Nellie clear up the table an' do up these dishes."

She bustled about. Marty wasn't sure what she was doing. She was aware only of the movement about her as she sat limp and uncaring.

Sally returned, carrying a slightly rumpled tiny figure, who, in spite of her sleepiness, managed a happy smile. Marty noticed only the smile and the deep blue eyes that looked at her, stranger to the little one. This must be Missie, she thought without feeling. This was verified when Clark stepped through the door and the girl welcomed him with a glad cry and outstretched arms. He swept her up against his chest and for a moment placed a cheek against hers. Then, thanking his host and hostess, he turned to let Marty know that they'd be on their way.

Mrs. Graham walked out with her. There were no congratulations or well-wishing on the new marriage. No one had made an attempt to make an occasion of it, and Marty breathed a sigh of relief for that. One misplaced word, no matter how sincerely spoken, would have broken her reserve and caused the tears to flow, she was sure. But none had been spoken. Indeed, the marriage was not even mentioned. These pioneer people were sensitive to the feelings of others.

They said good-bye only as one neighbor to another, though Mrs. Graham's eyes held a special softness as she looked up at Marty and said simply. "I'll 'llow ya a few days to be settlin' in an' then I'll be over. It'll be right nice to have another woman so close to hand to visit now an' then."

Marty thanked her and the team moved forward. They were again at the mercy of the dusty road and the hot sun.

"There it be—right over there." Marty almost jumped at Clark Davis' words, but she lifted her eyes to follow his pointing finger.

Sheltered by trees on the north and a small rise on the west, was the homestead that belonged to this man beside her.

A small but tidy cabin stood apart, with a well out front and a garden spot to one side. A few small bushes grew along the path to the door, and even from the distance Marty could see colors of fall blooms still upon them.

Off to one side was a sturdy log barn for the horses and cattle, and a pig lot stood farther back among a grove of trees. There was a chicken house between the barn and the house and various other small buildings scattered here and there. She supposed that she must learn the purpose for each one of them all in good time. Right now she was too spent to care.

"It's nice," she murmured, surprising herself, for she hadn't intended to say any such thing. Somehow, in her mind, it looked so much like the dreams that she and Clem had shared, and the knowledge hurt her and made her catch her breath in a quiet little sob. She said nothing more and was relieved when Missie, seeing her home, took all of her pa's attention in her excitement.

When they pulled up at the front of the house, a dog came running out to meet them and was greeted affectionately by both Clark and Missie.

Clark helped Marty down and spoke gently. "Ya best git ya in out of the sun and lay ya down a spell. Ya'll find the bedroom off'en the sittin' room. I'll take charge a Missie an' anythin' else thet be a needin' carin' fer. It's too late to field work today anyway."

He opened the door and held it while she passed into this strange house that was to be her home, and then he was gone, taking Missie with him.

She didn't bother to look around her but, feeling that she must lie down or else collapse, she made her way through the kitchen and found the door off the sitting room that led to the bedroom. The bed looked inviting and she stopped only long enough to slip her feet from her shoes before falling upon it. It was cooler in the house and her tired body began to demand first consideration over her confused mind. Sobs overtook her, but gradually her seething emotions subsided enough to allow her to sink into deep, yet troubled, sleep.

Chapter 3

Marriage of Convenience

Marty awoke and looked out the window. She was surprised to see that it was already dusk outside. Vaguely aware of someone stirring about in the kitchen, the smell of coffee and bacon made her realize that she was hungry. She heard Missie's chatter and remembered again why she was here. Without caring about anything, she arose, slipped on her shoes and pushed her hair back from her face. She supposed that she was a mess, but what did it matter? She was surprised in the dim light to see her trunk sitting against the wall by a chest of drawers. Everything that she owned was in there; even that thought failed to stir her.

She opened the trunk, took out her brush and ran it through her hair. Then she rummaged for a ribbon and tied her hair back from her face. At least she had made some improvement, she hoped. She smoothed her wrinkled dress and headed toward the smell of the coffee. Clark looked at her inquiringly as she entered the room, then motioned her to a chair at the table.

"I'm not much of a cook," he said, "but it be fillin'."

Marty sat down and Clark came from the stove with a plate of pancakes and another of side bacon. He set it down and went back for the steaming coffee. She felt a sense of embarrassment as she realized that he was doing what she should have been doing. Well, it would be the last time. From now on she'd carry her load. Clark sat down, and just as Marty was about to help herself to a pancake she was stopped short by his voice.

"Father, thank ya fer this food ya provide by yer goodness. Be with this, yer child, as Comforter in this hour, an' bless this house an' make it a home to each one as dwells here. Amen."

Marty sat wide-eyed looking at this man before her, who spoke, eyes closed, to a God that she did not see nor know—and him not even a preacher. Of course she had heard of people like that, who had a God outside of church, who had a religion apart from marryin' an' buryin', but she had never rubbed elbows, so to speak, with one before. Nor did she wish to now, if she stopped to think about it. So he had a God. What good did it do him? He'd still needed someone to help with his Missie, hadn't he? His God didn't seem to do much about that. Oh, well, what did she care? If she remembered right, people who had a God didn't seem to hold to drinkin' an' beatin' their women. With a little luck maybe she wouldn't have to put up with that anyway. A new wave of despair suddenly overwhelmed her. She knew nothing about this man. He could be anything! Maybe she should be glad that he was religious. It might save her a heap of trouble.

"Aint ya hungry?"

His words made her jump and she realized that she had been sitting there letting her thoughts wander.

"Oh, yeah, yeah," she stammered and helped herself to the pancake that he was holding out to her.

Missie ate with a hearty appetite, surprising in one so tiny, and chattered to her father, at the same time. Marty thought that she picked out a word or two here and there, but she really didn't put her mind to understanding what the child was saying.

After the meal she heard herself volunteering to wash up the dishes and Clark said fine; he'd see to putting Missie to bed then. He showed her where things were and then, picking up Missie, he began washing and readying her for bed.

Marty set to work on the dishes. As she opened doors and drawers of another woman's cupboards, a strange sense of uneasiness settled on her. She must force herself to get over this feeling she knew, for she had to take over this kitchen like it belonged to her. She couldn't restrain the slight shudder that ran through her, though.

As she returned from emptying her dishwater on the rose bush by the door, Clark was pulling a chair up to the kitchen table.

"She be asleep already," he said.

Marty placed the dishpan on its peg and hung the towel on the rack to dry. What now? she wondered, but he took care of that for her.

"The drawers in the chest all be empty. I moved my things to the lean-to. Ya can unpack an' make yerself more comfortable like. Feel free to be a usin' anythin' in the house, an' if there be anythin' thet ya be a needin', make a list. I go to town most Saturdays fer supplies, an' I can be a pickin' it up then. When ya feel more yerself like, ya might want to come along an' do yer own choosin'.

"I think thet ya better git ya some sleep. It's been a tryin' day. I know thet it's gonna take ya some time to stop a hurtin'—fer ya to feel at home here. We'll try not to rush ya."

Then his gaze demanded that she listen and understand. "I married ya only to have Missie a mama. I'd be much obliged if ya 'llow her to so call ya."

It was an order; she could feel it as such. But her eyes held his steadily, and though she said nothing, her pride challenged him. Okay! She knew her place. He offered her a place of abode; she in turn was to care for his child. She'd not ask for charity. She'd earn her way. Missie's mama she would be. She turned without a word and made her way to the bedroom. She closed the door behind her and stood for a few moments leaning against it. When she felt more composed she crossed quietly to where she could look down on the sleeping child. The lamp gave a soft glow, making the wee figure in the crib appear even smaller.

"All right, Missie," Marty whispered, "let's us make a deal. Ya be a good kid an' I'll do my best to be a carin' fer ya."

She looked so tiny and helpless there and Marty realized

that here, at less than two years of age, was someone that life had already hurt. What deserving thing had this little one done to have the mother that she loved taken from her? Marty's own baby stirred slightly within her, and she placed a hand on the spot that was slowly swelling for the world to know that she was to be a mother. What if it were my little one, left without my care? The thought made near panic take hold of her. Again she looked at the sleeping child, her brown curls framing her pixie face, and something stirred within her heart. It wasn't love that she felt, but it was a small step in the right direction.

Marty was up the next morning as soon as she heard the soft click of the door as Clark left the house to go to the barn. Quietly she dressed so as not to disturb Missie, and left the room, determined to uphold her part of the 'convenience' marriage of which she found herself a part. So she had a roof over her head. She'd earn it. She would be beholden to no man, particularly this cold individual whose name she now shared. She refused, even in her thoughts, to recognize him as her husband. And speaking of names, she cautioned herself, it wasn't going to be easy to remember that she was no longer Martha Claridge, but Martha Davis. Listlessly she wondered if the law would object if she stubbornly clung to her 'real' name. Surely she could be Martha Lucinda Claridge Davis without incriminating herself. Then with a shock she realized that her baby would have the Davis name too.

"Oh, no!" she stopped short and put her hands to her face. "Oh, no, please. I want my baby to have Clem's name."

But even as she fought it and let hot tears squeeze out between her fingers, she knew that she'd be the loser here as well. She was in fact married to this man, no matter how unwelcome the thought; and the child who would be born after the marriage would be in name his, even if it was Clem's. She felt a new reason to loathe him.

"Well, anyway, I can name my baby Claridge iffen I want to," she declared hotly to herself. "He can't take thet from me."

She brushed her tears on her sleeve, set her chin stubbornly, and went on to the kitchen.

The fire was already going in the big black cookstove, and Marty was glad that she wouldn't have to struggle with that on top of her almost insurmountable task of just carrying on. She opened the cupboard doors and searched through tight sealed cans until she found the coffee. She knew where the coffee pot was, she thought thankfully. Hadn't she washed it and put it away herself? There was fresh water in the bucket on a low table near the door and she had the coffee on in very short order.

"Well, thet's the first step," she thought. "Now what?"

She rummaged around some more and came up with sufficient ingredients to make a batch of pancakes. At least that she could do. She and Clem had almost lived on pancakes, the reason being that there had been little else provided for her to prepare. She wasn't going to find it an easy task to get proper meals, she realized. Her cooking had been very limited. Well, she'd learn. She was capable of learning, wasn't she? First she'd have to discover where things were kept in this dad-blame kitchen. Marty rarely used words that could be classed as profane, though she had heard plenty in her young lifetime. She sure felt like turning loose a torrent of them now, though. Instead she chose one of her father's less offensive expressions—about the only one that she had been allowed to use.

"Dad-blame!" she exploded again. "What's a body to do?"

Clark would expect more than just pancakes and coffee she was sure, but what and from where was she to get it?

There seemed to be no end of tins and containers in the cupboards, but they were all filled with ingredients, not something for breakfast.

Chickens! She'd seen chickens, and where there were chickens there should be eggs. She started out to go in search of some, through the kitchen door, through the shed that was the entry attached to the kitchen, when her eye caught sight of a strange contraption at the side of the shed. It looked like some kind of pulley arrangement and following the rope down to the floor she noticed a square cut in the floor boards and one end had a handle attached. Cautiously she approached, wondering if she might be trespassing where she did not belong. Slowly she lifted the trap door by the handle. At first she could see nothing; then, as her eyes became more accustomed to the darkness, she picked out what appeared to be the top of a large wooden box. That must be what the pulley and rope were for. She reached for it and began to manipulate the ropes, noticing that the box appeared to be moving upward. It took more strength than she had guessed it would, yet she found that she could handle it quite nicely.

Slowly the box came into view. She could feel the coolness that accompanied it. At last the box was fully exposed and she slipped the loop of rope over a hook that seemed to be for that purpose. The front of the box was fitted with a door, mostly comprised of mesh, and inside she could see several items of food. She opened the door and gasped at the abundance of good things. There were eggs in a basket, crocks of fresh cream, milk and butter, side bacon and ham. On the next shelf were some fresh vegetables and little jars containing preserves and, of all things, she decided after a quick sniff, fresh honey. Likely wild. What a find! She'd have no problem with breakfast now. She took out the side bacon and a few eggs. Then she chose some of the jam and was about to lower the box again when she remembered Missie. The child should have milk to drink as long as it was plentiful, and maybe Clark liked cream for his coffee. She didn't know. In fact, she didn't know much at all about the man.

Carefully she lowered the box again and replaced the trap door. Gathering up her find, she returned to the kitchen feeling much better about the prospect of putting breakfast on the table.

The coffee was already boiling and its fragrance reminded her how hungry she was. She took the dishes from the cupboard and set the table. She'd want the food hot when Clark came from chores, and she didn't know how long they took him in the mornings.

Chapter 4

Morning Encounter

Marty had just turned back to mixing her pancakes when she heard Missie. Best get her up and dressed first, she decided, and left her ingredients on the cupboard. As she appeared at the bedroom door, Missie's bright smile faded away and she looked at Marty with surprise, if not alarm.

"Mornin', Missie," Marty said, and lifted the child from the crib to place her on her own bed.

"Now I wonder where yer clothes be?" She spoke to the child.

They were not in the large chest of drawers, for Marty had already opened each drawer when she unpacked her own things the night before. She looked around the room and spotted a small chest sitting beneath the room's one window. It was Missie's all right, and Marty selected garments that she felt suitable for that day. She did have some sweet things. Her mama must have been a handy seamstress.

Marty returned to the tiny one who sat wide-eyed, watching her every move. She laid the clothes on the bed and reached for Missie, but as the child realized that this stranger was about to dress her, she made a wild grab for her shoes and began screaming.

Marty decided her shrieks would pale a ghost.

"Now Missie, stop thet," she scolded, but by now the child was howling in either rage or fright, Marty knew not which.

"I wan' Pa," she sobbed.

Marty conceded defeat.

"Hush now, hush," she said, picking up the squirming little girl. Gathering the clothes against the heaving, howling child, she carried her to the kitchen, where she placed girl and belongings in a corner. Missie pulled her clothes to her possessively, still sobbing as she did so. Marty turned back to the pancakes just as the coffee sputtered and boiled over. She made a frantic grab for the pot, pulling it farther to the back of the stove. She'd put in too much wood, she realized. The stove was practically jumping with the heat. She looked around for something with which to clean up the mess, and finding nothing that seemed suitable, went to her own room where she pulled a well-worn garment from her drawer. The thing was not much more than a rag anyway she decided, and back she went to the kitchen to mop up. Missie howled on. It was to this scene that Clark returned. He looked from the distraught Marty, who had by now added a burned finger to the rest of her miseries, to the screaming Missie in the corner, still clinging furiously to her clothes.

Marty turned from the stove. She had done the best that she could for now. She tossed the soggy, smelly garment into the corner and her eyes sparked as she nodded toward Missie.

"She wouldn't let me dress her," she stormed. "She jest set up a howlin' fer her pa."

She wasn't sure how she expected Clark to respond, but certainly not as he did.

"I'm afeared a child's memory is pretty short," he said evenly, so calmly that Marty blinked.

"She already be a fergettin' what it's like to have a mama."

He moved toward the cupboard, not even glancing Missie's way lest it encourage her to a fresh burst of tears.

"She'll jest have to learn thet ya be her mama now an' thet ya be boss. Now ya take her on back to the bedroom an' git her dressed an' I'll take over here." He indicated the somewhat messy kitchen and the partially prepared breakfast. Then he crossed and opened a window to let some of the heat from the roaring stove escape, and did not look at either Marty or Missie again.

Marty took a deep breath and stooped to scoop up Missie who reacted immediately with screams like a wounded thing, kicking and lashing out as she was carried away.

"Now look you," Marty said through clenched teeth, "remember our bargain? I said be ya good, I would be yer mama, an' this ain't bein' good." But Missie wasn't listening.

Marty deposited her on the bed and was shocked to hear Missie clearly and firmly state between screams, "I—wan'—Mama."

So she did remember. Marty's cold anger began to melt slowly. Maybe Missie felt about her the way she did about Clark—angry and frustrated. She didn't really blame her for crying and kicking. She would be tempted to try it herself had not life already taught her how senseless and futile it would be.

"Oh, Missie," she thought. "I knows how ya be feelin'. We'll have to become friends slow-like, but first—" she winced, "first, I somehow has to git ya dressed."

She arranged the clothes in the order that she would need them. There would be no hands to sort them out as she struggled with Missie, she knew. Then, she sat down and took the fighting child on her knee. Missie still threw a fit. No, it wasn't fear. Marty could sense that now. It was sheer anger on the child's part.

"Now Missie, ya stop it."

Marty's voice was drowned out by the child's and then Marty's hand smacked hard, twice, on the squirming bottom. Perhaps it was just the shock of it, or perhaps the child was aware enough to realize that she was mastered. At any rate her eyes looked wide with wonder and the screaming and squirming stopped. Missie still sobbed in noisy, gulping breaths, but she did not resist again as Marty dressed her.

When the battle was over, the child dressed, and Marty exhausted and dishevelled, the two eyed one another cautiously.

"Ya poor mite," Marty whispered and pulled the little thing close. To her surprise, Missie did not resist, but cuddled close, allowing herself to be held and loved as they rocked gently back and forth. How long they sat thus Marty did not know, but gradually she realized that the child was no longer sobbing. Detecting the smell of frying bacon coming from the kitchen, she roused herself and used her comb, first on her own unruly hair, and then on the child's brown curls. She picked up Missie and returned to the kitchen, dipping a cloth in cool water to wash away the child's tears and also to cool her own face. Clark did not look up. There he was, doing what she should be doing again, Marty thought dejectedly. The pancakes were ready, the eggs fried, the bacon sizzling as he lifted it from the pan. The coffee steamed in their cups and a small mug of milk sat at Missie's place. There was nothing left to do but to go sit down. He brought the bacon and sat down across from her.

She wouldn't be caught this time. She remembered that he prayed before he ate, so she bowed her head and sat silently. She sat quietly waiting. Nothing happened—then she heard faint stirrings—like the sound of pages being turned. She stole a quick glance upward and saw Clark sitting, Bible in hand, turning the pages to find the place that he wanted. She could feel the color rising slowly to her cheeks but Clark did not look up.

"We read today, Psalm 121," he said and began to read.

" 'I will lift up mine eyes unto the hills from whence cometh my help.' "

Marty wished solemnly that her help would come from the hills. In fact, she'd take it from any direction. She brought her mind back to catch up to Clark's reading. She had already missed some by letting her mind wander.

" 'The Lord is thy keeper: the Lord is thy shade upon thy right hand.

" 'The sun shall not smite thee by day, nor the moon by night.

" 'The Lord shall preserve thee from evil: he shall preserve thy soul.

" 'The Lord shall preserve thy going out and thy coming in from this time forth and even for evermore.' "

Gently he laid the book aside on a small shelf close to the table, and then, as he bowed his head and prayed, Marty was caught off-guard again.

"Dad-burn him," she thought, but then her attention was taken by his words.

"Our God, fer this fine day an' yer blessin's we thank ya."

"Blessin's," thought Marty. "Like a howlin' kid, spilled coffee an' a burned finger. Blessin's?"

But Clark went on.

"Thank ya, Lord, thet the first hard mile with Missie be travelled, an' help this one who has come to be her new mama."

"He never calls me by my name when he's a talkin' to his God," thought Marty, "always 'this one.' If his God is able to be answerin' his prayers, I sure hope He knows who he's talkin' 'bout. I need all the help thet I can git."

Marty heard the rattle of dishes and realized that her mind had been wandering and she had missed the rest of the prayer, including the Amen, and still she sat, head bowed. She flushed again and lifted her head, but Clark was fixing Missie's pancake so her embarrassment went unobserved.

At first breakfast was a quiet meal. Missie was too spent from her morning battle to be chattery and Clark seemed preoccupied. Marty, too, sat with her own thoughts and they were not at all pleasant ones.

"What after breakfast?" she wondered.

First she'd have to do up the dishes, then properly clean the messy stove. Then what? She'd love a chance to wash up the few pitiful things that comprised her wardrobe. She'd also like to wash the blankets that she had, and pack them away in her trunk. She'd need them again when she joined the wagon train going east.

Her mind wandered on, making plans as to how she might repair the few dresses that she possessed if she could just find a little bit of cloth some place. Clark said he went to town on Saturdays. This was Wednesday. She'd have to take stock of the cupboards and try to have a list ready for him. She stole a glance at him and then quickly looked back at her plate. He certainly did not look like a happy man, she told herself. Brooding almost, one could call it. At any rate deep-looking, as though trying to sort through something.

Then Missie cut in with a contented sigh, and a hearty, "All done, Pa." She pushed her plate forward. The face was transformed.

"Thet's Pa's big girl," he beamed, and the two shared some chattering that Marty made no effort to follow. Clark rose presently and refilled his coffee cup, offering her more too. Marty scolded herself for not noticing the empty cup first.

Clark pushed back his plate and took a sip of the hot coffee. Then he looked evenly across at her. She met his gaze, though she found it difficult to do so.

"S'pose ya be at a loss, not knowin' where to find things an' all. I see ya found the cold pit. Good! There be also a root cellar out back. Most of the garden vegetables are already there. Only a few things still be out in the garden. A shelf with cannin's there too, but ya need a light along to do yer choosin'; it be dark in there. There's also a smoke house out by the root cellar. Not too much in it right now. We plan on doin' our fall killin' and curin' next week. Two of the neighbors and me works together. There be chickens—fer eggs an' fer eatin'. We try not to get the flock down too low, but there's plenty to spare right now. There won't be fresh meat until it turns colder, 'ceptin' fer a bit of the pork. When the cold weather comes we try an' get some wild game; it keeps then. Sometimes we kill us a steer if we think we be a needin' it. There be fish in the crik too. When the work is caught up I sometimes try my hand at loafin' an' fishin'. We're not bad off, really."

It was not a boast, simply a statement.

"We have us real good land and the Lord be blessin' it. We've had good crops fer the last four seasons. The herd has built up too and the hogs an' chickens are plentiful enough. All the garden truck thet we can use can be growed right out aside the house an' there's lots of grain in the bins fer seedin'.

"We has some cash—not much, but enough an' iffen we do be needin' more, we can always sell us a hog.

"We're better off than a lot of folks, but the neighbors

round about here are makin' good too. Seems as how our move to the West been a good one.

"Got me some cuttin's a few years back from a man over acros't the crik; an' in a couple of years, if all goes well, we should have some fruit on 'em. The apples might even be a settin' next year, he tells me.

"I'm a tellin' ya this so's ya be knowin' the lay-o-the-land, so to speak. Ya don't need to apologize fer askin' fer what ya be a needin', both fer yerself an' fer Missie. We've never been fancy but we try an' be proper."

He pushed back from the table after his long speech, and stood silently for a moment, as if sorting out in his thinking if there was anything else that he should tell her.

"We has a couple a good milk cows a milkin' at present an' another due with an' off-season calf, so we have all the milk an' butter we be needin'.

"There's a good team of horses an' a ridin' horse too, iffen ever ya want to pay a visit to a neighbors. Ma Graham be the closest, an' she's 'bout as good company as anybody be a wantin'. I think ya'll find her to yer likin' even if she be a lot older than you.

"Most of my field work is done fer the fall, but I do have me a little breakin' I aim to do yet, iffen winter holds off awhile. First, though, I plan to spend a few days helpin' one o' the neighbors who ain't through yet. He got 'im a slow start. Plan to go over there today—Jedd Larson—an' give 'im a hand. I'll be asked to stay to dinner with 'em so won't be home 'til chore time. Ya can make yerself to home an' you an' Missie git to know one another like, an' maybe we won't have anymore of those early mornin' fusses."

He turned to Missie then and swung her up easily into his arms.

"Ya wanna come with Pa to git ole Dan an' Charlie?"

She assented loudly and the two set off for the barn.

Marty stirred herself. No more early mornin' fusses. That was his only reference to the incident. He hadn't seemed to pay much heed at the time, but, she reflected, maybe it had bothered him more than he let on.

She began to clear the table. Clark had said so much that it seemed difficult to sort out at one time. She'd shelve it for now and draw on it later as she had need. She began to make plans for her day.

She'd scout around and find a tub to heat water and then wash clothes and blankets as she had hoped she could. Maybe she'd be able to find a needle and thread and do the much needed repair work as well.

By the time she had started on the dishes, Clark was back to deposit Missie, working to detach her clinging arms. Missie had by now become used to going everywhere with her pa, and it wasn't going to be easy for the first while to make her understand that things would be different now.

After Clark had left and Missie had finally ceased her crying, Marty put away the last of the dishes and set to work cleaning the stove. That done, she swept up the floor and felt ready to turn to her own plans for the day.

She had never had much practice at keeping a real house, but she was determined that she would do a good job of it. Clark was never going to be embarrassed about the home that he lived in as long as she was earning her way. As soon as she had her own things in order, she'd turn her attention to the house, which had been a bachelor's quarters for too long. Even though Clark had been better than most in keeping things up, still it wasn't as a woman would have it. Just give her a few days. She'd have things in order.

Chapter 5

Iffen I Can Jest Stick It Out . . .

By late afternoon Marty had finished washing everything that belonged to her and some of Clark's and Missie's clothes as well. The day was much cooler than the previous one, she thought with relief. She couldn't have tolerated another one like that. This felt more like mid-October, even if it was still a glorious Indian summer day.

Marty looked out toward the west. Far beyond the rolling hills the blue mountains rose in majesty. Was it from here that Clark was seeking the help of his God?

The trees along the hillside were garbed in yellows and reds. Indeed, many of the leaves were already on the ground or being carried southward by a gusty breeze.

It was a beautiful scene and how happy she would have been to share it with Clem. If only she and Clem could have had this together. Her heart ached even more than her tired back as she emptied the water from the washtubs.

Missie was having a nap. Marty was glad to be free of the child for a while—almost as glad as she had been to have Clark away for the day. How relieved she had felt at his announcement that morning. Maybe with luck the neighbor's work would keep him away for several days. She hardly dared hope for so much. She had planned to look around the farm today to learn where things were, but she felt far too tired just now. She'd just sneak a few minutes of rest while Missie was still sleeping and then take her scouting trip a little later.

She threw out the last of the rinse water, replaced the tubs on the pegs on the side of the house and with extreme weariness went in to stretch out on her bed. She cried a bit before sleep claimed her, but the sleep that came was the most restful one that she'd had since Clem had died.

Marty slept on, unconscious of the fact Missie had awakened, looked over at her as she slept, and then, with a great deal of maneuvering, climbed from her crib and went in search of her pa.

Marty awoke with a start—not sure what had roused her, but already sensing that something was wrong. Maybe Missie had cried. She propped herself on one elbow and looked at the crib. No, it wasn't that. Missie wasn't even there. Missie wasn't there? But she must be.

Marty sprang up, her heart pounding. Where was Missie? Maybe Clark had come home and taken the child with him.

"Don't panic," she told herself. "She's got to be okay."

Marty checked the corral but the team was not back. She looked all around the buildings, calling as she went. No Missie. She ranged farther and farther from the buildings but still no Missie. She was getting frantic now in spite of her efforts to keep herself under control. Where could Missie be? What should she do?

Tears were streaming down Marty's cheeks. Her dress had suffered another tear near the hem and she had thorns in her hands from the wild rose bushes that she had forced her way through. She checked the creek—up and down its banks, searching the clear, shallow water, but no sign of Missie or of anything that belonged to her.

Maybe she followed the road, Marty thought, and she set off at a hurried pace down the dusty, rutted roadway. On and on she stumbled. Surely she couldn't have gone this far, Marty reasoned, but she hurried on because she knew of nothing else to do. Then, over the hill in the road ahead she saw Clark's team coming toward her.

She could have stopped by the side of the road and waited

for him to approach her, but she did not even think of it.

What could she say to Clark? How could she tell him? She could not even be trusted to care for one small child. Would Clark have some idea of where to search for her that Marty had not already tried?

On she plodded until finally she had to step aside to allow the team to draw up beside her. She looked up at Clark, misery showing on her dirt and tear-streaked face—there sat Missie as big as life on her pa's knee, looking very proud of herself.

Clark whoaed the horses to a stop and reached down a hand to help Marty into the wagon. She climbed up reluctantly, her head spinning. Oh, what must he think? They travelled toward home in silence. Why didn't he say something? He'd not spoken since he'd said giddup to the team. Missie was quiet too. Well, she'd better be, the little demon. If she said one word, Marty knew she'd feel like smacking her. Her great relief at seeing her safe and sound was now replaced with a feeling of anger toward the child. Marty's face stung, both from the effort of her frantic search and her deep humiliation. Then her chin went up. So he wasn't talking. Well—neither was she. He could think what he would, she wasn't doing any explaining. She hated him anyway and she didn't think much more of his undisciplined child.

"Iffen I can jest stick it out fer thet wagon train, then I'll be a goin' out of this wretched place so fast ya won't even find my tracks."

The woman in her wanted desperately to resort to tears, but the woman in her also refused her even that small comfort.

"Don't ya dare," she warned herself, "don't ya dare give him thet satisfaction."

She held her head high, eyes straight ahead and remained that way until they reached the house. Contemptuously she ignored any help that Clark might have given her, and climbed down over the wheel, managing to tear her dress even farther.

He placed Missie on the ground and Marty scooped the child up rather roughly and went into the house. Missie seemed unbothered by it all and paid no attention as her new mama went noisily about starting another fire in the kitchen stove, the last one having died out.

Another meal to prepare—but what? It caused her further embarrassment, but Marty knew that it would have to be pancakes again. That was about the only thing that she really knew how to make. Well, let him choke on them. She didn't care. Why should she? She owed him nothing. She wished that she had stayed in her wagon and starved to death. That's what she wished.

Amazingly enough, Marty's fire started and the fine cookstove was soon spilling out heat. Marty didn't even think to be grateful as she stormed about the kitchen, making coffee and preparing her batch of pancake batter. She'd fry a few pieces of ham rather than bacon, she decided.

She really couldn't understand why it bothered her so much that all of her efforts since coming to this house had met with such complete failure. She shouldn't care at all, and yet she did—much as she didn't want to. Underneath, Marty felt deeply that failure was a foe to be combated and defeated. It was the way she had grown up and it was not easily forsaken now.

While the griddle was heating, she cast an angry look at Missie.

"Now you stay put," she warned, then hurried out to bring in all of her washing before the night's dampness set in.

When Clark came in from the barn, supper, such as it was, was ready. If he was surprised at pancakes again, he did not show it. Marty burned to realize that his pancakes had been just as good as hers.

"So what?" she stormed. "My coffee be okay."

It must have been too, because when she again missed seeing Clark's empty cup, and he got up to refill it, he remarked, "Good coffee," as he poured her second cup. Marty's face burned again.

After supper she cleared the table and washed Missie up for bed. She still felt like shaking the little tyke each time that she touched her but refrained from doing so.

When Missie had been tucked in and Marty had washed

her own hot, dusty feet, she excused herself with a murmur, and, gathering her things from a chair in the sitting room, took them to her bedroom and shut the door. It would soon be necessary to light the lamp. She carefully folded her worn dresses and undergarments, laying them on her bed. If only she had a needle and some thread. But she wouldn't ask him, she determined. Never!

She sat down on her bed to allow herself a more comfortable position for her self-pity. It was then that she noticed a small sewing basket in the corner behind the door. For a moment she couldn't believe her amazing find, but upon crossing to the basket she discovered more than she had dared to hope for.

There was thread of various colors, needles of several sizes, a perfect pair of scissors, and even some small pieces of cloth.

Determinedly Marty settled down. Sewing, now that was one thing that she could do. Though mending hardly fit into the same category as sewing, she felt.

She was dismayed as she tried to make something decent out of the worn things before her, and the longer she worked the more discouraged she became. She had attacked the least worn items first, but by the time she reached the last few articles she was completely dejected. They'd never last the winter and it was a sure thing that she'd never ask him for anything. Never! Even if she was forced to wear nothing but rags.

She remembered his words as she pulled the torn dress over her head and replaced it with a mended nightie.

"We've never been fancy, but we try an' be proper."

"Well, Mr. Proper, what could ya do when ya had nothin' to make yerself proper with?"

Marty fell into bed, and as the events of the day crowded through her mind—the spilled coffee, the tantrum-throwing Missie, the frantic search, more pancakes—a sob arose in her throat, and again she cried herself to sleep. If Clem were only there, her world would be made right again.

Chapter 6

Housecleanin'

The next morning showed a cloudy sky as Marty looked out of the window. The weather was changing. It wouldn't be long until the beautiful Indian summer would have to give way to winter's fury, but not yet, she told herself. The day was still warm and the sky not too overcast. Perhaps the clouds would soon move away and let the sun shine again.

Slowly she climbed from her bed. Surely today must be an improvement on yesterday she hoped. Already yesterday seemed a long way in the past—and the day before—the day that she had buried Clem—. Marty could hardly believe that that had happened only two brief days ago. Two days that had seemed forever.

Marty slipped into the gingham that she had mended the night before, cast a glance in Missie's direction and quietly moved toward the door. She did hope that the early morning scene of yesterday would not be repeated. She didn't know if she could take it again.

She put on the coffee and set the dishes on the table, then started the preparations for the morning pancakes.

"Dad-blame it." She bit her lip. "I'm tired of pancakes myself."

It hadn't seemed so bad to have pancakes over and over when that was all that was available, but with so much good food at her disposal, it seemed a shame to be eating pancakes.

She'd have to figure something out, but in the meantime they needed breakfast. She went out for another piece of side bacon.

Missie awoke and without incident allowed Marty to dress her. Score one point for that! She placed her in the homemade chair and pulled it back from the table to keep small fingers from pulling things off.

When Clark came in from the barn the breakfast was ready and Missie sat well behaved in her chair. Clothed and in her right mind, Clark mused. He did not bother to say it aloud, for he feared that the context would be missed by Marty.

They sat down together at the table and after the morning reading and prayer, breakfast proceeded without anything out of the ordinary happening.

Marty watched carefully, even though on the sly, for the emptying of Clark's coffee cup, but when she jumped for the pot he waved it aside.

"I'd like to but I'd better not take me a second cup this mornin'. The sky looks more like winter every day an' Jedd still has him some grain out. I'm gonna git on over there as quick as I can—" he hesitated "—but thet's good coffee."

Marty poured her own second cup and put the pot back. The only thing that he could say about her was that she made good coffee. Well, maybe she was lucky that she could do that much!

Clark stopped at the door and said over his shoulder. "I'll be eatin' my dinner with the Larsons agin." Then he was gone.

This time Missie's complaining lasted only a few minutes. Marty's thoughts turned to his words. "Bet he's tickled pink to be able to have 'im one meal a day to the Larsons. Wouldn't it be a laugh should Missus Larson give 'im pancakes."

In spite of herself Marty couldn't keep a smile from flitting across her face. Then she sat down to leisurely enjoy her second cup of coffee and plan her day.

First she would completely empty and scrub out the kitchen cupboards and then she'd go on to the rest of the kitchen, the walls, window, curtains. By night, she vowed, everything would be shining.

She didn't spend as long over her coffee as she had intended, for, as she planned her day, she became anxious to begin it.

She hurriedly washed up the dishes and found Missie some things that she hoped would keep her amused for a while. Then she set to work in earnest. She might lack in a lot of ways, she thought, but she could apply herself—and apply herself she did.

By the time the ticking clock on the mantle told her that it was twelve-thirty, the cupboards were all scrubbed and rearranged to suit her own fancy. She had discovered things too, like ground corn for muffins and grains for cooked cereals. Maybe breakfast wouldn't always have to be pancakes after all.

She stopped and prepared a meal for herself and Missie, consisting of fried ham and a slice of bread, with milk to drink for both of them. She was glad that milk was plentiful. Clem had fretted that she should be drinking milk for the baby on the way. Now there was milk in abundance, and Clem's boy would be strong when he arrived.

After Marty tucked Missie in for her nap, she set to work again. She felt tired but under no circumstances would she lie down and give Missie a chance to repeat her performance of yesterday. The little tyke must have walked over a mile before she met her pa. At the thought of it Marty felt again the sting of humiliation. No sirree, there was no way that she would let that happen again even if she dropped dead on her feet.

On she worked, washing the curtains and placing them out in the breeze to dry. Then she tackled the window until it shone, and went on to the walls with more energy than she knew she possessed. It was hard, slow work, but she was pleased with her accomplishment. As she scrubbed away at the wooden walls she was amazed at the amount of water that it took. A number of times she had to stop and refill her pan. Remembering the curtains, she stopped her scrubbing and went in search of anything resembling an iron so that she could press the curtains before rehanging them. She found a set of sad irons in the shed's corner cupboard and placed them on the stove to heat. It was then that she realized that in her preoccupation with her scrubbing, she had let the fire go out again, so the task of rebuilding it was hers once more. She scolded herself as she fussed with the small flame to try to coax it into a blaze. When finally it began to sustain itself she returned to her scrubbing. She refilled her pan many more times and had to take the buckets to the well for more water. Finally the task was finished. The logs shone even if they had 'drank' water.

By the time she brought in the curtains the irons were hot enough to press them. They looked fresh and crisp as she placed them at the window.

Missie wakened and Marty brought her from her bed and got a mug of milk for each of them. Missie seemed cheerful and chattery after her sleep and Marty found her talkative little companion rather enjoyable. It kept her mind off other things—just as her hard work had been doing.

She placed Missie in her chair with a piece of bread to nibble on and set to work on the wooden floor with hot soapy water and scrub brush. By the time she was through, her arms and back ached, but the floor was wondrously clean. She gave the rug at the door a good shaking outside and replaced it again, then stood and surveyed the small kitchen. Everything looked and smelled clean. She was proud of herself. The kitchen window gleamed, the curtains fairly crackled with cleanness, the wall—the walls looked sort of funny somehow. Oh, the logs looked clean and shiny but the chinking—somehow the chinking looked strange, sort of gray and muddy instead of the white it had been before.

Marty crossed to the nearest wall and poked a finger at the chinking. It didn't just look muddy. It *was* muddy—muddy and funny. Marty wrinkled her nose. What had she done? The water of course! It wasn't the logs drinking the water, the chinking had slurped up the scrub water thirstily and now it was gooey and limp. She hoped with all of her heart that it would dry quickly before Clark got home. She looked at the clock. It wouldn't be long either. She'd better get cracking if supper was to be more than pancakes.

She had noticed that the bread was as good as gone; then what would she do? She had never baked bread before nor even watched her mother do it that she could remember. She hadn't the slightest idea how to start. Well, she'd make biscuits. She didn't know how to bake them either, but surely it couldn't be too hard. She washed her hands and went to the cupboard. She felt that it was more 'her' cupboard, now that she had put everything where she wanted it.

She found the flour and salt. Did you put eggs in biscuits? She wasn't sure, but she'd add a couple just in case. She added milk and stirred the mixture. Would that do it? Well, she'd give it a try.

She sliced some potatoes for frying and got out some ham. She supposed that she should have some vegetable too, so she went to work on some carrots. As she peeled them she heard Ole Bob welcome home the approaching team. Clark would care for the horses and then do the chores. He'd be in for supper in about forty minutes, she guessed, so she left the carrots and went to put the biscuits in the oven. They handled easily enough and she pictured an appreciative look in Clark's eyes as he reached for another one.

She went back to her potatoes in the frying pan, stirring them carefully so that they wouldn't burn.

"Oh, the coffee!" she suddenly cried and hurried to get the coffee pot on to boil. After all, she could make good coffee!

She sliced some ham and placed it in the other frying pan, savoring the aroma as it began to cook. She smelled the biscuits and could barely refrain from opening the oven door to peek at them. She was sure they'd need a few minutes more. She stirred the potatoes again and looked anxiously at the muddy chinking between the logs. It wasn't drying very fast. Well, she wouldn't mention it and maybe Clark wouldn't notice it. By morning it would be its old white self again.

The ham needed turning and the potatoes were done. She pulled them toward the back of the stove and put more wood in the fire box. Then she remembered the carrots. Oh, dear, they were still in the peeling pan, only half ready. Hurriedly she went to work on them, taking a small nick out of a finger in her haste. Finally she had the pot of carrots on the stove, placing them on what she hoped was the hottest spot to hurry them up.

The potatoes were certainly done, rather mushy looking from being over-cooked and over-stirred, and now they sat near the back of the stove looking worse every minute. The biscuits! Marty grabbed fiercely at the oven door, fearing that the added minutes may have ruined her efforts, but the minutes had not ruined them at all. Nothing could have done any harm to those hard-looking lumps that sat stubbornly on the pan looking like so many rocks.

Marty pulled them out and dumped one on the cupboard to cool slightly before she made the grim test. She slowly closed her teeth upon it—to no avail; the biscuit refused to give. She clamped down harder; still no give.

"Dad-burn," murmured Marty, and opening the stove she threw the offensive thing in. The flames around it hissed slightly, like a cat with its back up, but the hard lump refused to disappear. It just sat and blackened as the flame licked around it.

"Dad-blame thing. Won't even burn," she stormed and crammed a stick of wood on top of it to cover up the telltale lump.

"Now, what do I do with these?"

Marty looked around. How could she get rid of the lumpy things? She couldn't burn them. She couldn't throw them out to the dog to be exposed to all eyes. She'd bury them. The rotten things. She hurriedly scooped them into her skirt and started for the door.

"Missie, ya stay put," she called. Then remembering her previous experience, she turned and pulled the coffee pot to the back of the stove.

Out the door she went, first looking toward the barn to make sure that her path was clear. Then quickly she ran to the far end of the garden. The soil was still soft and she fell on her knees and hurriedly dug a hole with her hands and dumped in the disgusting lumps. She covered them quickly and sprinted back to the house. When she reached the yard, she could smell burning ham.

"Oh, no!" she cried. "What a mess!"

She washed her hands quickly at the outside basin, and the tears washed her cheeks as she raced for the tiny kitchen where everything seemed to be going wrong.

When Clark came in for supper, he was served lukewarm mushy potatoes and slightly burned slices of ham along with the few slices of bread that remained. There was no mention of the carrots which had just begun to boil, and of course no mention of the sad lumps called biscuits. Clark said nothing as he ate. Nothing, that is, except, "That's right good coffee."

Chapter 7

A Welcome Visitor

Friday was clear and bright again though the air did not regain the warmth of the first part of the week. Marty had made no comment on the muddy chinking, but as they had eaten their supper the night before one small chunk in the corner had suddenly given way and lost its footing between the logs, falling to the floor, leaving a bit of a smear behind it. Clark had looked up in surprise, but then had gone on eating. Marty prayed, or would have prayed had she known how, that the rest of it would stay where it dad-burn belonged. It did, and she thankfully cleared the table and washed the dishes.

The light was needed now, as the days were short, and the men worked in the fields as late as they could before turning to chores. Marty was glad when darkness fell that night. The lamplight cast shadows obscuring the grayish chinking. As she washed Missie for bed, she thought that she heard another small piece give way, but she refused to admit it, raising her voice to talk to Missie and try to cover the dismaying sound.

That had been last night, and as Marty faced this new day she wondered what dreadful things it held for her. One thing she knew. The bread crock was empty and she had no idea at all of how to go about refilling it. She supposed that Clark knew how to bake bread, but she'd die before she'd ask him. And what about the chinking? Had the miserable stuff finally dried to white and become what it was supposed to be? She dreaded the thought of going to look, but lying there wasn't going to solve any problems.

She struggled up from her bed. Her muscles still ached from her strenuous efforts of the day before. She'd feel it for a few days she was sure. Besides, she hadn't slept well. Her thoughts had again been on Clem and how much she missed him. Now she dressed without caring, ran a comb through her hair and went to the kitchen.

The first thing that she noticed was the chinking. Here and there all around the walls, small pieces had given way and lay crumbled on the floor. Marty felt like crying, but little good that would do. She'd have to face Clark with it, confess what she had done and take his rebuke for it.

She stuffed a couple more sticks of wood on the fire and put on the coffee. Suddenly she wondered just how many pots of coffee she would have to make in her future. It seemed at the moment that they stretched out into infinity.

She found a kettle and put on some water to boil. This morning they'd have porridge for breakfast. But porridge and what? What did you have with porridge if you had no biscuits, no muffins, no bread, "no nuthin'," Marty fretted and, pulling the pot off angrily, went to work again making pancakes.

Missie awakened and Marty went in to pick her up. The child smiled and Marty found that she returned it.

"Mornin', Missie. Come to Mama," she said, trying the words with effort to see how they'd sound. She didn't really like them she decided, and wished that she hadn't even used them.

Missie came gladly and chattered as she was being dressed. Marty could understand more of the chatter now. She was saying something about Pa, and the cows that went moo, and the chickens that went cluck, and pigs—Marty couldn't catch the funny sound that represented the pigs, but she smiled at the child as she carried her to her chair.

Clark came in to a now familiar breakfast and greeted his daughter who squealed a happy greeting in return.

After the reading of the Word, they bowed their heads for Clark's prayer. He thanked his Father for the night's rest and the promise of a fair day for the layin' in of the rest of Jedd's harvest.

Marty was surprised at the next part of the prayer.

"Father, be with the one who works so hard to be a proper mama for Missie, an' a proper keeper of this home."

The prayer went on but Marty missed it. Everything that she had done thus far had been a flop. No wonder Clark felt that it would take help from the Almighty himself to set things in order again. She didn't know if she should feel pleased or angry at such a prayer, so she forcefully shoved aside the whole thing just in time for the Amen.

"Amen," echoed Missie, and breakfast began.

At first they ate silently, Clark and Missie exchanging some comments and Clark scolding Missie.

"Don't ya be a throwin' pancake on the floor. Thet's a naughty girl an' makes more work fer yer mama."

Marty caught a few other references to 'yer mama' as well, and realized that Clark had been using the words often in the past two days. She knew that he was making a conscious effort at educating the little girl to regard her as mama. She supposed she'd have to get used to it. After all, that was what she was here for—certainly not to entertain the serious-looking young man across the table from her. Another piece of chinking clattered down and Marty took a deep breath and burst forth.

"I'm afeared I made a dreadful mistake yesterday. I took on to clean the kitchen—"

"I'd seen me it was all fresh and clean lookin' an' smellin'," Clark cut in.

Now why'd he do that, she stormed? She took another gulp of air and went on.

"But I didn't know what scrub water would be a doin' to the chinkin'. I mean, I didn't know thet it would all soak up like, an' then not dry right agin."

Clark said nothing. She tried again.

"Well, it's fallin' apart like. I mean—well, look at it. It's crumblin' up an' fallin' out—"

"Yeah," said Clark, not even lifting his eyes.

"Well, it not be stayin' in place," Marty floundered. "Whatever can we do?"

She was almost angry by now. His calmness unnerved her. He looked up then, and answered slowly.

"Well, when I go to town on Saturday, I'll pick me up some more chinkin'. It's a special kind like. Made to look whiter an' cleaner, but no good at all fer holdin' out the weather—the outside chinkin' has to do thet job. There still be time to re-do it 'fore winter sets in. Water don't hurt the outer layer none, so it's holdin' firm like. Don't ya worry yerself none 'bout it. I'm sure thet the bats won't be a flyin' through the cracks afore I git to 'em."

He almost smiled and she could have gleefully kicked him. He rose to go.

"I reckon ya been pushin' yerself pretty hard though, an' it might be well if you'd not try to lick the whole place in a week like. There's more days ahead an' ya be lookin' kinda tired." He hesitated. "Iffen ya should decide to do more cleanin', jest brush down the walls with a dry brush. Okay?"

He kissed Missie good-bye and, telling her to be a good girl for her mama, went out the door for what he said might be the last day of helping Jedd Larson with his crop. She supposed he'd be around more then. She dreaded the thought, but it was bound to come sooner or later.

She put water on to heat so that she could wash up the rag rugs before winter set in, and then found a soft brush to dust the sitting-room walls.

It didn't take nearly as long to brush them as it had to scrub the kitchen, and it did take care of the cobwebs and dust. She was surprised to be done so quickly and did the windows and floor as well.

The washed curtains were still fluttering in the fall breeze and the rugs drying in the sun when she heard the dog announce a team approaching. Looking out of the window she recognized Mrs. Graham, and her heart gave a glad beat as she went out to welcome her. They exchanged greetings and Ma put her team in the shade and gave them some hay to make them more content to wait. Then she followed Marty to the house.

The dog lay to one side of the path now, chewing hard on a small bonelike object. Marty saw with horror that it was one of her biscuits. The dad-blame dog had dug it up. With a flush to her cheeks she hurried Mrs. Graham by, hoping that the older woman would fail to recognize the lump for what it really was.

As they entered the kitchen, Marty was overcome with shyness to a degree that she had never faced before. She had never welcomed another woman into her kitchen. She knew not what to do nor what to say, and she certainly had nothing at all to offer this visitor.

Ma Graham kept her eyes discreetly from the crumbled chinking and remarked instead about the well-scrubbed floor.

Marty bustled about self-consciously, stuffing wood in the stove and putting on the coffee. Ma talked easily of weather, and Missie and the good harvest. Still Marty felt ill at ease. She was thankful when the coffee had boiled and she was able to pour them each a cup. She placed Missie in her chair with a glass of milk and put on the cream and sweetening for Ma in case she used it. With a heavy heart she realized that she didn't have a thing to serve with the coffee—not so much as a crust of bread. Well, the coffee was all that she had, so the coffee would have to do.

"I see ya been busy as a bee, fall cleanin'." Ma observed.

"Yeah," responded Marty. She wanted it done before winter shut her in.

"Nice to have things all cleaned up fer the long days an' nights ahead when a body can't be out much. Them's quiltin' an' knittin' days."

Yeah, that's how she felt.

"Do ya have plenty of rugs fer comfort?"

She was sure that they did.

"What 'bout quilts? Ya be needin' any of those?"

No, she didn't think so.

They slowly sipped their coffee. Then Ma's warm brown eyes turned upon her.

"How air things goin', Marty?"

It wasn't the words, it was the look that did it. The look in Ma's eyes said that she truly cared how things were going, and Marty's firm resolve to hold up bravely went crumbling just like the chinking. Words tumbled over words as she poured out to Ma all about the pancakes, Missie's stubborn outburst, the bread crock being empty, the horrid biscuits, Missie's disappearance, the chinking, the terrible supper that she had served the night before, and, finally her deep longing for the man whom she had lost so recently. Ma sat silently, her eyes filling with tears. Then suddenly she rose and Marty was fearful that she had offended the older woman by her outburst, but Ma felt no such thing. She was a woman of action and truly she could see that action was needed here.

"Come, my dear," she said gently. "You air a gonna have ya a lesson in bread makin'. Then I'll sit me down an' write ya out every recipe thet I can think of. It's a shame what ya've been a goin' through the past few days, bein' as young as ya are an' still sorrowin' an' all, an' if I don't miss my guess"—her kind eyes going over Marty—"ya be in the family way too, ain't ya, child?"

Marty nodded silently, swallowing her tears, and Ma took over, working and talking and finally managing to make Marty feel more worthwhile than she had felt since she had lost her Clem.

After a busy day Ma departed. She left behind her a reef of recipes with full instructions, fresh baked bread that filled the kitchen with its aroma, a basket full of her own goodies and a much more self-confident Marty with supper well under control.

Marty breathed a short prayer that if there truly was a God up there somewhere, He'd see fit to send a special blessing upon this wonderful woman whom she had so quickly learned to love.

Chapter 8

It's a Cruel World

Saturday dawned clear and cooler and breakfast of porridge and corn muffins was hurried so that Clark might get an early start to town. Marty presented him with the list that Ma Graham had helped her with the day before.

"Mind ya," said Ma, "in the winter months it be sometimes three or four weeks between the trips we be a takin' to town because of winter storms, an' ya never know ahead which Saturdays ya be a missin' so ya al'ays has to be stocked up like."

So the list had been a lengthy one and Marty inwardly felt concern, but Clark did not seem surprised when she handed it to him and he read quickly through it to be sure that he had no questions concerning it. He kissed Missie good-bye, promising her a surprise when he returned, and was gone.

Marty sighed in relief to again have a day without him about, and turned her thoughts to planning what she would do with it. Clark had warned her to take things a bit easier, and Ma Graham said that she feared that she was 'overdoin' for a woman in her state, but Marty knew that she must have something demanding to fill her hours or her sense of loss would overwhelm her. So she looked round about her to see what to tackle on this day. She'd finish her cleaning, she decided. First she'd put water on to heat so that she could wash the bedding. Then she'd do the window, walls and floor in the bedroom and, if time still allowed, she'd do the shed. She did not even consider cleaning the lean-to. That was Clark's private quarters she felt, and she would not trespass.

All day she worked hard, forcing her mind to concentrate on what she was doing. A dull fear raised its head occasionally. If she finished all of the hard cleaning today, what would she do tomorrow, and tomorrow and tomorrow? Marty pushed it aside. The tomorrows would have to care for themselves. She couldn't handle that right now. She was sure that if she let her mind fix on that, she'd break under the weight of it.

She finished her final task of the day just in time to begin her supper preparations. Clark had said that he should be home for the usual chore time. She thumbed through the recipes that Ma had left. She'd fix biscuits and a vegetable stew, she decided, using some of the meat broth that Ma had brought to flavor the stew. She went to work, discovering that she had forgotten the fire again.

"Dad-burn it. Will I never learn?" she fretted, as she set to work to rebuild it.

The vegetables were simmering when she heard the team. Clark unhitched the wagon near the house to make it easier for the unloading of the supplies, and went on down to the barn with the horses.

Marty continued her supper preparations. This time, thanks to Ma Graham, the biscuits looked far more promising.

She noticed that Clark looked weary when he came in from his chores. He gave Missie a hug before he sat down at the table, but Marty thought that his shoulders seemed to sag a bit. Was shopping really that hard on a man, or had she made the list too long, and spent all of his money? As she sat at supper Marty fretted over the problem but there didn't seem to be an answer, so she concentrated on cooling Missie's stew.

" 'Fraid the totin' in of all of the supplies will sort of mess up yer well-ordered house fer the moment." Clark's voice cut in on her thoughts.

"Thet's okay," Marty responded. "We'll git them in their proper place soon enough."

"A lot of the stock supplies will go up in the loft over the kitchen," Clark went on. "Ya reach it by a ladder on the outside of the house."

Marty's eyes widened in surprise.

"I didn't know there be a loft up there."

"It's nigh empty right now, so there wasn't much use in a knowin'. We stock it up in the fall, so's we won't run out of sech things as flour an' salt come the winter storms. I'll carry the stock supplies direct up, so's I won't have to clutter yer house with 'em. The smaller things though, I'll have to bring in here, so's ya can put 'em all away in the place where ya want 'em. Do ya be a wantin' 'em in the kitchen or in the shed?"

Marty knew that it would be handier in the kitchen, yet if they were in the shed, it wouldn't make such a clutter until she got them put away. She opted for the shed, and they hurried through their supper in order to get at the task.

After they had finished eating, Clark pulled from his pocket a small bag of sweets and offered one to Missie. Then he gave the sack to Marty, telling her to help herself, and then to tuck it up in the cupboard for future enjoyment. Missie smacked and sucked at the special treat, declaring it 'num' and Pa's 'yummy'.

As Marty washed the dishes Clark brought the supplies in to the shed so that she would have things there to work on as soon as she was free to do so.

As she filled cans and crocks to put them away Marty felt heady with the bounty of it all. She could hear Clark as he labored under the heavy bags, moving again and again up the ladder to the kitchen loft.

Marty found it necessary to finish the job by lamplight, but at last it was all done. The cupboards were bulging. Imagine if she and Clem could have stocked up like that. Wouldn't it have been like Christmas and picnics and birthdays all wrapped up in one? She sighed and wiped away an unbidden tear.

Marty was tucking Missie in for the night, wondering if Clark was going to hear her prayers as he usually did, when she heard him in the kitchen. He seemed to be struggling with a rather heavy load and Marty's curiosity led her back to investigate. She arrived to find Clark, hammer in hand removing a crate from some large object. She stood watching silently from the door while Clark's tool unmasked the crate's contents. Her breath caught in her throat, for there with shining metal and polished wood, stood the most wondrous sewing machine that she had ever seen.

Clark did not look at her, but began speaking. His voice sounded as weary as his shoulders had looked, but he seemed to feel that a brief explanation was in order.

"I ordered it some months back as a s'prise fer my Ellen. She liked to sew an' was al'ays makin' somethin' fancy-like. It was to be fer her birthday. She would have been twenty-one—tomorrow." Clark looked up then. "I'd be proud if ya'd consider it yourn now. I'm sure ya can make use of it. I'll move it into yer room under the window iffen it pleases ya."

Marty held back a sob. He was giving her this beautiful machine. She was speechless. She had always dreamed of having a machine of her own, but never had she dared to hope for one so grand. She didn't know what to say, yet she felt that she must say something.

"Thank ya," she mumbled. "Thank ya. Thet—thet'll be fine, jest fine."

Only then did she realize that the big man before her was fighting for control. His lips trembled and as he turned away she was sure that she saw tears in his eyes. Marty brushed by and went out into the coolness of the night. She had to think, to sort things out. He had ordered the machine for his Ellen, and he was weeping. He must be suffering, too. She had noted the weary sag of his shoulders, the quivering lips, the tear-filled eyes. Somehow she had never thought of him as hurting—of being capable of understanding how she felt. Hot tears washed down Marty's cheeks.

"Oh, Clem," her heart cried. "Why do sech things, sech cruel things, happen to people? Why? Why?"

But Marty knew that there was no easy answer. This was the first time that Clark had mentioned his wife. Marty hadn't even known her name. Indeed, she had been so wrapped up in her own grief that she had not even wondered much about the woman who had been Clark's wife, Missie's mama, and the keeper of this house. Now her mind was awake to it. The rose by the door, the bright cheery curtains, Missie's lovingly sewn garments that she was fast outgrowing, the many colorful rugs on the floor. Everything—everything, everywhere spoke of this woman. Marty felt suddenly like an intruder. What had she been like, this Ellen? Had she ever boiled the coffee over or made a flop of the biscuits? No, Marty was sure that she hadn't. But she had been so young— only twenty-one tomorrow—and she was already gone. True, Marty was even younger, nineteen in fact, but still twenty-one seemed so young to die. And why did she die? Marty didn't know. There were so many things that she didn't know, but a few things were becoming clear to her. There had been a woman in this house who loved it and made it a home, who gave birth to a baby daughter that she cherished, who shared days and nights with her husband. Then he had lost her and he hurt—hurt like she did over losing her Clem. She had been feeling that she was the only one in the world who bore that sorrow, but it wasn't so.

"It's a mean world," she thought as she turned her face upward. "It's mean an' wicked an' cruel," she stormed.

The stars blinked down at her from a clear sky.

"It's mean," she whispered, "but it's beautiful. What was it that Ma had said? 'Time' she'd said, 'it is time that is the healer—time an' God.'" Marty supposed that she meant Clark's God.

"Iffen we can carry on one day at a time, the day will come when it gets easier an' easier, an' one day we surprise ourselves by even bein' able to laugh an' love agin." That's what Ma had said.

It seemed so far away to Marty, but somehow she had the firm belief that Ma Graham should know.

Marty turned back to the house. It was cool in the evening now, and she realized that she was shivering. When she entered the kitchen she found that all traces of the machine and the crate had been removed.

On the kitchen table was a large package wrapped with brown paper and tied with store twine. Clark indicated it.

"I'm not sure what might be in there," he said. "I asked Missus McDonald at the store to make up whatever a woman be a needin' to pass the winter. She sent thet. I hope it passes."

Marty gasped. Just what did he mean? She wasn't sure.

"Would ya like me to be a movin' it in on yer bed so's ya can be a sortin' through it?"

Without waiting for her answer, which may have taken half the night, she felt so tongue-tied, he carried it through to her room and placed it on her bed. He turned to leave.

"It's been a long day," he said wearily. "I think I'll be endin' it now," and he was gone.

Marty's fingers fumbled as she lit the lamp. Then she hurried to try to untie the store string. Remembering the scissors in the sewing basket, she hastened to use them to speed up the process. She could hardly wait, but as the brown paper fell away she was totally unprepared for what she found.

There was material there for undergarments and nighties and enough lengths for three dresses. One piece was warm and soft-looking in a pale blue-gray; already her mind was picturing how it would look done up. It would be her company and visiting dress. It was beautiful. She dug farther and found a pattern for a bonnet and two pieces of material. One light weight and one heavier, for the colder weather.

There was lace for trimming, and long warm stockings, and even a pair of shoes, warm and high for the winter, and a shawl for the cool days and evenings, and on the bottom, of all things, a long coat. She was sure that no one else in the whole West would have clothes to equal hers. Her eyes shone and her hands trembled. Then with a shocked appeal to her senses, she pulled herself upright.

"Ya little fool," she muttered. "Ya can't be a takin' all this. Do ya know thet iffen ya did, ya'd be beholden to thet man fer years to come?"

Anger filled Marty. She wanted the things, the lovely things, but oh, she couldn't possibly accept them. Oh, what could she do? She would not humble herself to be 'beholden' to this man. She would not be a beggar in his home. Tears scalded her cheeks. Oh, what could she do? What could she do?

"We are not fancy, but we try an' be proper," haunted her.

Could it be that he was embarrassed by her shabbiness? Yes, she decided, it could well be. Again her chin came up.

Okay, she determined, she'd take it—all of it. She would not be an embarrassment to any man. She would sew up the clothes in a way that would be the envy of every woman around. After all, she could sew. Clark need not feel shame because of her.

But the knowledge of what she knew or thought that she knew, drained much of the pleasure from the prospect of the new clothes.

In his lean-to bedroom, Clark stretched weary, long legs under the blankets. It had been a hard day for him, fraught with difficult memories.

It used to be such fun to bring home the winter supplies to Ellen. She made such a fuss over them. Why, if she'd been there today she would have had Missie sharing in the game and half-wild with excitement. Well, he certainly couldn't fault Marty, only five days a widow. He couldn't expect her to be overly carried away about salt and flour at this point. She must hurt—she must really hurt. He wished he could be of some help to her, but how? His own pain was still too sharp. It took time, he knew, to get over a hurt like that, and he hadn't had enough time yet. The thought of wanting another woman had never entered his head since he'd lost Ellen. If it weren't for Missie, this one wouldn't be here now either; but Missie needed her even if he didn't, and one could hardly take that out on the poor girl.

At first he had resented her here, he supposed—cleaning Ellen's cupboards, working at her stove—but no, that wasn't fair either. After all, she hadn't chosen to be here. He'd just have to try harder to be decent and to understand her hurt. He didn't want Missie in an atmosphere of gloom all the time. No, he'd have to try to shake the feeling and in time maybe she could too, so that the house would be a fit place for a little girl to grow up in. It would be harder for her as she was all alone. She didn't have a Missie, or a farm, or anything really. He hoped that Mrs. McDonald had made the right choices. She really was going to need warmer things for the winter ahead. The thought that he was doing something special for her in getting her the things that she needed did not enter his thinking. He was simply providing what was needed for those under his roof, a thing that he had been taught was the responsibility of the man of the house. He had learned this when he was but a 'young 'un' tramping around, trying to keep up to the long strides of his own pa.

Chapter 9

The Lord's Day

Sunday morning dawned bright and warm with only enough clouds in the sky to make an appealing landscape. While at breakfast, Marty, hoping that she wasn't too obvious, asked Clark if he was through at Jedd's or would he be going back for the day. Clark looked up in surprise.

"Jedd has him a bit more to finish off," he said, "an' I wouldn't be none surprised iffen he'd work at it today. Me, though, I al'ays take a rest on the Lord's Day. I know it don't seem much like the Lord's Day with no meetin', but I try an' hold it as sech the best thet I can."

Now it was Marty's turn for surprise. She should have known better if she had given it some thought, but in her eagerness to get Clark from the house she hadn't considered it at all.

"Course," she whispered, avoiding his eyes. "I'd plumb fergot what day it be."

Clark let this pass and was silent for a moment. Then spoke.

"I been thinkin' as how me an' Missie might jest pack us a lunch an' spend the day in the woods. 'Pears like it may be the last chance fer a while. The air is gettin' cooler an' there's a feelin' in the air thet winter may be a mite anxious to be a comin'. We kinda enjoy jest spendin' the day lazyin' an' lookin' fer the last wild flowers, an' smart-lookin' leaves an' all. Would thet suit yer plans?"

She almost stuttered. "Sure—sure—fine. I'll fix yer lunch right after breakfast."

"Good!"

It was settled then. Clark and Missie would spend the day enjoying the outdoors and one another, and she, Marty, would have the day to herself. The thought both excited and frightened her.

Clark went out into the shed and returned with a strange contraption which appeared to be some sort of carrier to be placed on his back.

"Fer Missie." He answered the question in her eyes. "I had to rig this up when I needed to take her to the fields an' a chorin' with me. She even had her naps in it as I tramped along." He smiled faintly. "Little tyke got right heavy at times, too, fer sech a tiny mite. Reckon I'd better take it along today fer when she tires of walkin'."

Marty completed the packing of the lunch. She realized that she was giving them far more than they needed, but the fresh air and the walk through the hills was bound to give them a hearty appetite.

Missie was beside herself with excitement and called goodbye over and over to Marty as they left. Ole Bob joined them at the door and Marty watched the trio disappear back of the barn. She remembered as she turned back to clear the table and do up the dishes that today would have been Ellen's birthday. Maybe their walk would include a visit to her grave. Marty somehow believed that it would.

She hurried through the small tasks of the morning and then fairly bolted to her bedroom and the waiting material and shiny new machine. She wasn't sure if she was breaking Clark's sabbath with her sewing or not. She hoped not, but she was not sure that she could have restrained from doing so even if she had known. She did hope that she would not offend Clark's God. She needed any help that He was able to give. She pushed the thoughts aside and let her mind be completely taken up with her task—almost. At times she nearly caught her breath with feelings that came from nowhere.

"Wouldn't Clem be proud to see me in this?"

"This is Clem's favorite color."

"Clem al'ays did poke fun at what he called 'women's frivols'."

No, it seemed there was just no helping it. He was there to disquiet her thoughts even though his absence still made her throat ache. Stubbornly she did not give in to the temptation to throw herself on her bed and sob, but worked on with set jaw and determined spirit.

In the afternoon she laid her sewing aside. She hadn't even stopped for a bite to eat. She hadn't missed it, and her sewing had been going well. The machine worked like a dream and she couldn't believe how much faster seams were turned out with its help. She decided, however, that her eyes could use a rest. They had been staring at the machine foot for what seemed like years.

She walked outside. It was a glorious fall day and she almost envied Clark and Missie's romp through the crackling leaves. Slowly she walked around the yard. The rose bush had one single bloom—not as big or as pretty as the earlier ones, she was sure, but beautiful just for its being there. She went on to the garden. The vegetables for the most part had already been harvested. Only a few things remained to be taken to the root cellar. At the end of the garden was the hole that she had dug to bury her biscuits. It was re-dug by Ole Bob who had hastened to unearth them again. A few dirty hard lumps still lay near the hole. Even Ole Bob had abandoned them. It no longer mattered as much, thought Marty, giving one a kick with her well-worn shoe. Funny how quickly things can change.

She walked on, savoring the day. The fruit trees that Clark had told her of looked promising and healthy. Wouldn't it be grand to have your own apples? Maybe even next year, Clark had said. She stood by one of the trees, not sure if it was an apple tree or not, but should it be, she implored it to please, please have some apples next year. She then remembered that even if it did, by then she would have left for the East. She didn't bother to inform the apple tree of this, for fear that it would lose heart and not bear after all. She turned and left, not caring as deeply now.

On she walked, down the path to the stream just behind

the smoke house. She found that a stone platform had been built into the creek bed where a spring, cold from the rocky hillside, burst forth to join the waters below. A perfectly shaded spot was there to cool crocks of butter and cream in the icy cold water on hot summer days. Clark hadn't told her about this, but then there had been no reason to, it not being needed this time of year. She paused a moment, watching the gurgling water ripple over the polished stones. There was something so fascinating about water. She decided, as she pulled herself away, that this would be a choice place to refresh oneself on a sultry summer day.

She went on to the corrals, reaching over the fence to give Dan, or was it Charlie, a rub on his strong neck. The cows lay in the shade of the tall poplars, placidly chewing their cuds while their calves of that year grew fat on meadow grass in the adjoining pasture. This was a good farm, Marty decided—just what Clem and she had dreamed of having. Clem had no need of a farm now, and she, Marty?

She started for the house, past the henhouse, when she suddenly felt a real hunger for pan-fried chicken. She hadn't realized how long it had been since she had tasted any, and she remembered home and the rich aroma from her ma's kitchen. At that moment she was sure that nothing else would taste so good. Preparing chicken was one thing that she had watched her mother do. It had seemed to hold a fascination for her, and whenever they were to have fried-chicken she would station herself by her ma's kitchen table and observe the whole procedure from start to finish. Her mother had never had to begin with a live bird, though. Marty had never chopped a chicken's head off before, but she was sure that she could manage somehow.

She walked closer to the coop, eying the chickens as they squawked and scurried away, trying to pick out a likely candidate. She wasn't sure if she should catch the one that she wanted and take it to the axe or if she should go to the woodshed for the axe and bring it to the chicken. She finally decided that she would take the chicken to the axe, realizing that she would need a chopping block as well.

She entered the coop and picked out her victim, a young

cocky rooster that looked like he would make good frying.

"Come here you, come here," she coaxed him, stretching out her hand, but she soon caught on that a chicken would not respond like a dog. In fact, chickens were completely something else. They flew and squawked and whipped up dirt and chicken droppings like a mad whirlwind whenever you got to within several feet of them. Marty soon decided that if she was to have a chicken for supper, full pursuit was the only way to get one into the pan, so she abandoned herself to an outright chase, grabbing at chicken legs and ending up with a faceful of scattered dirt and dirty feathers. Round and round they went. By now Marty had given up on the cocky young rooster and had decided to settle for anything that she could get her hands on. Finally, after much running and grabbing, that had her dress soiled, her hair flying, and her temper seething, she managed to grasp hold of a pair of legs. He was heavier than she had expected, and it took all of her strength to hold him, for he was determined that he wasn't going to be supper for anyone. Marty held tight, just as determined. She half dragged him from the coop and looked him over. This was big-boy himself, she was sure, the granddaddy of the flock, the ruler of the place. So what, she reasoned. He'd make a great pan full, and maybe he hated the thought of facing another winter anyway.

Marty was panting with exhaustion as she headed for the woodshed, but felt very pleased with herself that she had accomplished her purpose.

She stretched out the squawking, flopping rooster across a chopping block and as he quieted, reached for the axe. The flopping resumed and Marty had to drop the axe in order to use both hands on the fowl. Over and over the scene was repeated. Marty began to think it was a battle to see who would wear out first. Well, it wouldn't be her.

"Ya dad-blame bird. Hold still," she hissed at him and tried again, getting in a wild swing at the rooster's head.

With a squawk and a flutter the rooster wrenched free and was gone, flopping and complaining across the yard. Marty looked down at the chopping block and beheld in horror the two small pieces of beak that remained there.

"Serves ya right!" she blazed and kicked the pieces off the block into the dirt.

She headed again for the coop, determined not to be beaten, while one short-beaked rooster still flapped about the farm, screaming out his insults to a dastardly world.

Marty marched resolutely to the coop and began all over again. After many minutes of chasing and gulping against the flying dust, she finally got what she was after. This fellow was more her size and again she set out for the chopping block. Things still didn't go well there. She stretched him out and reached for the axe, dropped the axe and stretched him out, over and over again. Finally she got inspired and taking the chicken with her, she headed for the house. Into her bedroom she went and took from a drawer the neatly wound roll of store string. Back to the wood shed she went, where she sat down on a block of wood and securely tied the legs of the chicken together. Then she carried him outside and tied the other end of the string to a small tree. Still holding the chicken, she tied another piece of string to his neck and stretching it out firmly tied the second string to another small tree. She then moved the chopping block from the woodshed and placed it in the proper spot beneath the chicken's outstretched neck.

"There now," she said, with some satisfaction, and taking careful aim she shut her eyes and chopped hard.

It worked—but Marty was totally unprepared for the next event, as a wildly flopping chicken covered her unmercifully with spattered blood.

"Stop thet! Stop thet!" she screamed. "Yer s'pose to be dead, ya—ya headless dumb thing."

She took another swing with the axe, relieving the chicken of one wing. Still it flopped and Marty backed up against the shed as she tried to shield her face from the awful onslaught. Finally the chicken lay still, with only an occasional tremor. Marty took her hands from her face.

"Ya dad-blame bird," she stormed, and wondered momentarily if she dared to pick it up.

She looked down at her dirty, blood-stained dress. What a mess, and all for a chicken supper.

Out in the barnyard an indignant short-beaked rooster

tried to crow as Marty picked up the sorry mess of blood and feathers and headed for the house.

All of those feathers had to come off, and then came the disgusting job of cleaning out the innards.

Somehow she got through it all, and after she had washed the meat in fresh well water and put it in seasonings, she put it on to simmer in savory butter. She decided that she'd best get cleaned up before Clark made his appearance. A bath seemed to be the the simplest and quickest way to care for the matter so Marty hauled a tub into her room and supplied it with warm water. When she was clean again she took the disgustingly dirty dress that she had been wearing and put it to soak in the bath water. She'd deal with that tomorrow, she promised herself as she carried the whole mess outside and placed it on a wash table beside the house.

Feeling refreshed and more herself after her bath, Marty went back to resume her preparations for supper. When Clark and Missie returned, tired but happy from a day spent together, they were greeted by the smell of frying chicken. Clark felt surprise but tried not to show it. Indeed, he was on the verge of asking Marty if she'd had company that day, so sure was he that she must have had help to accomplish such a thing, but he checked his tongue.

On the way to the barn to milk the cows, he saw the mess by the woodshed. The chopping block was still where Marty had left it, though Ole Bob had already carried away the chicken's head. The store twine was there too, still attached to the small trees.

As he passed the coop he noticed the general upheaval there as well. It looked like the chickens had flopped in circles for hours, feathers and dirt were everywhere, including the overturned feeding troughs and watering pans.

What really topped all was the old rooster perched on the corral fence with his ridiculously short beak clicking in anger.

"Well, I never," muttered Clark.

He couldn't help but smile at the sight of that rooster. Tomorrow he'd do something about him. Tonight he planned to enjoy fried chicken.

Chapter 10

Neighborly Hog Killin'

A new week began. Marty mentally braced herself for it, hoping with all of her heart that it would be packed full of activity.

Monday morning, true to the promise made the night before, Clark brought in the big rooster beheaded and plucked. He advised Marty to boil rather than try to fry the patriarch of the flock and Marty was glad to take his advice. After caring for the bird and putting him on to cook in her largest pot, Marty set to work washing up all of the clothing that she could find that needed washing. Her back ached from the scrub board, and she was glad to spend the rest of the day at her sewing.

The rest of the week was packed full, too. She went with Clark to Ben Grahams for the killing of the hogs. Todd Stern and his near-grown son, Jason, were there, too, and Marty recognized them as the kind neighbors who had brought Clem home and supplied his burying place. The pain was there, sharp and hurting again, but she made a real effort to push it from her. She was glad to be with Ma Graham. She seemed to draw so much strength from the older woman.

As the day went on, Marty could not help but notice the looks that were exchanged between young Jason and Ma's Sally Anne. If she didn't miss her guess, something was a brewin' there.

She had little time to ponder on it, however, for the cutting and preparing of the meat was a big job. After the menfolk had done the killing and the scraping, and had quartered the animals, the women were hard pressed to keep up with them.

The job that Marty found hardest to stomach was the emptying and preparing of the casings for the sausage meat. Floods of nausea swept over her, and several times she had to fight for control. When they were finally done, Marty went to the outhouse and lost all of her dinner. She was glad to be rid of it and went back to work feeling some better.

The men looked after preparing the salt brine for the curing of the bacon and hams and readied the smoke house for the process. The women ground and seasoned the sausage meat and had the slow, rather boring, task of stuffing the casings and tying them into proper lengths. It helped to be able to chat as they worked; still the job seemed a tedious one. On the second and third days, Hildi Stern came with her menfolk, and the extra hands aided much in getting the job done.

Lard had to be chopped up and rendered, some kept for cooking and frying and some put aside to be used in the making of soap.

At the end of each day those involved were tired and aching. Marty noticed that Ma tried to assign her the less demanding tasks, but she would have none of it, wanting to do her full share.

At the end of the third day things were cleaned up and put away for the next year's killing. The dividing up that could be done was taken care of and the rest marked for later use.

Ma's Sally Anne put on the coffee for them all to renew their strength for the work that waited at home at day's end. Marty noticed Jason look in Sally's direction and saw her face flush beneath it. She couldn't fault Jason. Sally Anne was a very pretty seventeen-year-old, and just as sweet as she was pretty, Marty thought. Was Jason good enough for her? Marty hoped so. She knew nothing of the boy to make her think otherwise. He looked strong and he certainly had been carrying his share of the work the last few days. He seemed mannerly enough. Yes, she summed it up—maybe he'd be all right.

Anyway, it looked like he'd have to be, the way they were mooning over one another.

She remembered again how it had been when she had first met Clem—his eyes on her and her cheeks flushed in her excitement. She had known right away that she would love him and she guessed that he had known it too. His very presence had sent fireworks through her. She couldn't wait to see him again, but she could hardly bear it when she did. She had thought she'd explode with the intensity of it, but that's what love was like. Wild and possessing, making one nearly burst with excitement and desire—being both sweet and cruel at the same time. That's how love was.

Clark was excusing himself from the table and Marty got up too. She said the necessary words to Ma Graham and eyed the crocks of lard that she was to take home for soap-making, when Ma Graham spoke.

"No use us both gittin' ourselves in a mess makin' soap. Marty, why don't ya leave them crocks here an' come over in the mornin' an' we'll do it all up together-like?"

Bless ya, Ma Graham, Marty's heart cried. Ya know very well I'd be downright lost on my own tryin' to make soap fer the first time.

She looked at Clark for his reaction.

"Good idee," Clark responded.

"Thank ya, Ma," Marty said with feeling. "I'll be over in the mornin' jest as soon as I can."

Thank you seemed very inadequate, but what else could she say?

Chapter 11

Togetherness

Marty kept her word and hurried through the morning household chores so that she could do her rightful share of the work at Ma's. As she went for Missie's coat and bonnet, Clark spoke up.

"I've nothin' pressin' to take my time today. Thought I'd be a doin' the caulkin' here in the kitchen. Why don'cha jest leave Missie to home with me an' then ya won't need to worry ya none 'bout her gittin' under foot around those hot pots."

Marty expressed her appreciation and agreement and hurried to the team and wagon that Clark had waiting.

It was cooler today. In fact, there was almost a chill to the air. Maybe winter would soon be coming. Marty hated the thought of those long days and even longer evenings that stretched out before her.

The soap-making went well, even though it was a demanding hot job and Marty was glad when they finished. It was then placed in pans ready to be cut into bars after it had cooled.

They sat down for a much needed cup of coffee and one of Ma's slices of johnny-cake. There was never much chance for confidential talking at Ma's house. What with a family of eleven crowding every corner of the small house, there was seldom an opportunity to be alone. But Ma talked freely, ignoring the coming and going.

She told Marty that her first husband, Thornton Perkins, had been the owner of a small store in town and when he had come to an early death, he had left her with the business to try to wrest a living from and three small children to care for. When Ben Graham came along with good farm land and the need for a woman, he appeared to be the answer to prayer even though he had four small ones tagging along behind him. So they had joined forces, the young widow with three and the widower with four. To that union had been born six more children. One they had lost as a baby and one at the age of seven. The seven-year-old had been one of Ma's, and Ben had felt the loss deeply. Now the children numbered eleven and every one of them was special.

Sally Anne and Laura were both seventeen, only two months apart, with Ben's Laura being the older of the two. Next came Ben's Thomas, then Ma's Nellie. Ma's Ben had been next and Ma supposed that one of the reasons Ben had become so attached to this boy was that they both bore the same name. Ben's twins were next in line, Lem and Claude. They were named after their two grandfathers. The younger children Marty still didn't have sorted out by name. There was a Faith and a Clint she knew and she believed that she had heard the little one called Lou.

It was the two older girls that most interested Marty. Sally Anne was one of the prettiest young things that she had ever seen and seemed to simply adore her step-sister Laura. Laura, though capable and efficient, was plain and probably knew it, for she seemed to always be indirectly trying to outdo Sally Anne. "Why does she do it?" Marty puzzled. "Can't she see that Sally Anne practically worships her? She has no earthly reason to lord it over her." In watching more closely she decided that Laura was unaware of what she was doing, but was driven by a deep feeling of being inferior to her pretty sister.

"She doesn't need to feel thet way," Marty reasoned. "She has so much to offer jest the way she be."

She supposed that there was nothing that she could do about it. However, she promised herself that she'd try to be especially nice to Laura and maybe make her realize that she was a worthwhile person.

It was getting to be late afternoon and Marty knew that she must be on her way.

She thanked Ma sincerely for all of her help with the soap. Now she felt confident that she'd be able to do it on her own the next time. She told Ma that if she could spare the time, she'd sure appreciate another visit from her before the snow shut them in. Ma promised to try, and giving Marty a hearty hug, sent her on her way.

When Marty reached home Clark met her to take the team, taking Missie with him for the brief trip to the barn. As she entered the kitchen she saw that all of the old crumbled chinking had been replaced with the new, and was rapidly turning to the proper attractive white. Now she wouldn't be sweeping up broken pieces each time that she swept the kitchen. She was glad that it was done, and noted with appreciation that Clark had even cleaned up any mess that he had made in the doing of the job.

Marty was tired as she began the supper preparations and would be very glad to go to bed. Tomorrow was Saturday, so she must first make a list for Clark as he would want to leave early for town the next morning.

Chapter 12

Finishin' My Sewin'

Clark did leave early for town the next day, and Marty sighed with relief as she watched him go. She still felt him a stranger to be avoided; though, without realizing it, some of her anger was seeping away simply because, deep down, she realized that it was unfounded. They were victims of circumstances, both of them, forced to share the same house. Notwithstanding, Marty was much relieved when his duties took him elsewhere.

The list hadn't been as long this time, but Clark had asked her to check through Missie's things to see what the child would be needing for the winter. Marty did this and carefully added the items to the list. Then Clark stood Missie on a chair and traced a pattern of her small foot so that he might bring her back new shoes.

Marty busied herself with her morning routine. She still felt tired. In fact she wondered if the emotionally-driven hard work of the preceding days was not taking its toll. She felt drained and even slightly dizzy as she finished up the dishes. For the sake of her little one, she must hold herself in check and not pour all of her energy into frenzied activity. She had lost her Clem. Now, more than ever, she wanted his baby.

Marty decided that she would make this day an easier one. She did her household chores for the day, sweeping and tidying each small room. Her bedroom had become quite crowded with the two beds, two chests, her trunk, the sewing basket and the new machine. She wouldn't complain, she thought, as she looked at the beautiful shining thing. There really was more room for it in the sitting room, but she was sure that for Clark to have to see it continually would be a hurtful reminder. No, she'd be glad to spare him that much, and she ran a loving hand over the polished wood.

"Today, Missie," she spoke to the child, "I'm a gonna finish my sewin'."

She crossed to the garments that she had already made and fingered them with pride. There hung the newly made bonnets, one of light material, a little more fussy, the other of warm sturdy cloth for the cold days ahead. There were the underclothes, some with bits of lace. She had never had such feminine things before. She almost hated to wear them and thus take away their newness. Two nighties lay folded in the drawer. She had put extra tucks and stitching on them and one had some dainty blue trim. Two dresses hung completed. They were not fancy, but they were neat and attractive, and Marty felt confident that Clark would have to deem them 'proper.'

Beside her chest stood the new shoes, still black and shiny. She had not as yet worn them. As long as she could she would wear her old ones and keep the new ones to admire. Her new coat and shawl hung on pegs behind the door, so very new, so new and beautiful.

Marty sighed. She had only the blue-gray material to make up. She had saved it until last because it was to be special. She let the beautiful material lie against her hand, then lifted one corner to her cheek.

"Missie," she half whispered, "I'm gonna make me a dress. Ya jest wait to see it. It gonna be so grand, an' maybe—maybe when I be all through, there be enough material left to make ya somethin' too."

Suddenly that was important to Marty. She wanted, with all of her heart, to share this bit of happiness with someone, and Missie seemed the likely one to share it with.

Missie patted the material and proclaimed it pretty.

Marty went to work. Missie played well on the rug by the bed, and the sewing machine hummed along. The morning went speedily, and when Missie became restless Marty was shocked to find that the clock said ten past one.

"Oh dear!" Marty exclaimed, picking up the child. "Missie, I'm plumb sorry. It be long past yer dinner time. Ya must be starvin'. I'll git ya somethin' right away."

They ate together and then Marty tucked Missie in for her nap. The child fell asleep listening to the dreamy whirr of the new machine.

The new dress took shape, and when she had carefully finished each tuck and seam, Marty held it up. It nearly took her breath away. She was sure that she had never had one quite so pretty. She couldn't resist trying it on and frankly admired herself. She removed it reluctantly and carefully hung it with her other dresses, arranging each fold to hang just right.

Eagerly she set to work on the small garment for Missie. She decided to make a small shirt from the white material that was left over from her underthings, with a jumper from the blue-gray wool.

The shirt was soon completed and with great care Marty set to work on the tiny jumper. The tucks were fussed over to make sure that they were just so, and each seam was sewn with utmost care. When Marty was finished she made small stitching across the yoke with needle and thread.

Missie, who had long since awakened from her nap, kept demanding to see the "pretty," and Marty's work would be interrupted while she showed her.

Suddenly Marty jumped from her chair as she heard Ole Bob welcoming Clark home.

"Dad-burn," she said, hastily laying her sewing aside and hurrying to the kitchen. "I haven't even thought me about supper."

The stove was cold to her touch. She had forgotten all day to nourish it.

Clark had driven down by the barn. The supplies would not take as many trips to carry this time, nor would they be as heavy to tote.

Marty fluttered about the kitchen. She remembered an old secret of her ma's. If your menfolk come looking for their supper and you are caught off guard, quickly set the table. That will make them think that supper is on the way.

In a mad flurry, Marty hastened to throw on the plates and cutlery. Then she flushed at her foolishness. That wouldn't fool Clark. He had a good forty minutes of choring ahead and wouldn't be looking for plates on yet. A stove with a fire in it might be a bit more convincing. When Clark came in, Marty was building the fire and wondering what she could have ready for supper in a little more than half an hour.

After depositing his armload of purchases, Clark went back out to do the chores and Marty set to work in earnest preparing the supper.

When Clark returned from the barn the meal was ready, simple though it was. Marty made no apology. After all, she told herself, it wasn't as though she had loafed away the whole day. Nevertheless, she promised herself to never let it happen again.

After the supper dishes had been cleared away, Clark brought forth his purchases for Missie. She went wild in her excitement, hugging the new shoes, jumping up and down about the new coat and bonnet, and running around in circles, waving the new long stockings in the air. She exclaimed over the material to be sewn into little frocks, but Marty was sure that the tiny child didn't really understand what it was all about. She returned to the shoes, pulled her bonnet on her head, back to front, and whirled another long stocking. Marty couldn't help but smile, knowing how the little girl felt.

Suddenly Missie turned and headed for the bedroom, a pair of the new stockings streaming out behind her. She's going to put them in her chest, Marty thought. In a moment the flying feet came running back and one of the tiny hands carried over her head the jumper that Marty had been working on. Marty watched as Missie pushed the garment onto Clark's lap, pointing at the fancy stitching and exclaimed, "Pretty. Mine. Pretty."

Clark gingerly picked up the small article in his big work-roughened hands. His eyes softened as he looked across at Marty. She held her breath. For a moment he did not speak but sat lightly stroking the small garment. In a somewhat choked voice he responded. "Yeah, Missie, very pretty," but it was to Marty that he spoke, not the excited child.

Clark had more surprises too. For Missie he had a picture book. She had never beheld such a thing before and spent the rest of the evening carefully turning the pages, exclaiming over and over the wonder of finding cows and pigs and bunnies in such an unlikely place. Clark had bought himself some books for the long winter evenings ahead, too. This was the first time Marty was aware that he was a reader. She then remembered the shelf in the sitting room with a number of interesting-looking books on it.

Clark had a package for her as well that would help pass the months ahead. It contained wool and knitting needles, and pieces of material for quilt piecing, and he had a sack of raw wool that he had stored in one of the outside buildings until such time as it was needed.

Marty was very thankful. She loved to knit and though she had never tried, she was willing to try her hand at quilting as well.

Missie was too excited to go to bed, but with a firmness that surprised Marty, Clark informed her that she had had enough excitement for one night and all of her things would be there in the morning. After Marty washed the child and got her ready for bed, Clark tucked her in and heard her short prayer. Marty carefully folded the new things and picked up the pieces of material. This would care for a few more days, she thought with relief. If only she could keep herself busy, perhaps she wouldn't hurt so much. She placed it all in Missie's chest for the night, planning to go to work on sewing the little garments on the morrow.

"Oh, no," she thought. "Tomorrow be another Lord's Day!"

She couldn't expect Clark and Missie to tramp off for two Sundays in a row.

"Dad-burn!" she exclaimed.

How in the world would she be able to suffer through the long, miserable day anyway? Maybe she should take to the woods. Well, tomorrow would have to care of itself. No use fretting about it now. She had a small amount of work to do yet on the jumper, and then she'd take her tired self off to bed. It seemed a usual thing these days for her to feel weary.

Chapter 13

Ellen

Sunday was a cool day with a wind blowing from the west. After the morning reading and prayer Marty's mind kept staying with the scripture. Clark was still reading from the Psalms, and Marty often found herself puzzled over some of the words. She was listening more closely now, and she often felt herself wanting to ask Clark to repeat slowly some portion so that she might ponder over its meaning.

Could Clark's God be a comfort to others like He had been to the writer David? Marty acknowledged that she knew very little about Clark's God and sometimes she caught herself yearning to know more; Bible reading hadn't been a part of her upbringing. She wondered in a vague way if she had missed something rather important. On occasion Clark would give a few words of his own as a background or setting to the scripture for that day, telling a bit about the author and his troubled life at the time of his writing. Marty knew that the words were for her understanding, but she didn't resent it. Indeed, she drank it in as one thirsting for knowledge.

This morning, as Clark prayed, Marty found herself wondering if she dared to approach Clark's God in the direct way that Clark himself did. She felt a longing within her to do so but she held back.

When Clark said Amen, Marty's lips also formed the words.

Breakfast began after Missie declared her loud 'Amen,' too.

"What air we gonna do with this long day afore us?" Marty thought. She knew that today she could not sew. She had defied Clark's God in so doing once, but to repeat it would be tempting His anger to fall upon her and she couldn't risk that. If He had any help at all that He could spare for her, she desperately needed it.

Clark interrupted her thoughts.

"On the way to town yesterday, I stopped me at the Grahams to see if there be anythin' thet I might be gettin' them in town. Ma asked thet we come fer a visit an' dinner today. Who knows how many nice Sundays we be a havin' afore winter sets in? I said I'd check with ya on it."

"Bless ya, Ma," thought Marty. "Oh, bless ya, Ma."

Out loud she said, quite calmly, "I'd be a likin' thet," and it was settled.

She hurried with the morning dishes and when Clark went to get the team ready, she hastened to get Missie and herself ready to go.

She dressed Missie in the new shirt and jumper with a pair of the new stockings and the little black shoes. She brushed out Missie's curls until they were light and fluffy. The child truly did look a picture as she twirled and pirouetted, admiring herself.

Marty then turned to her own dresses. She took the new blue-gray one from the hanger, but couldn't bring herself to wear it. It should have been for Clem, that dress, and somehow she just couldn't put it on to accompany Clark. If he failed to notice it, she would be hurt, and if by some strange chance his eyes showed admiration, that would hurt even more. She didn't want admiration from him or any other man. She could still see clearly Clem's love-filled eyes as he pulled her to him. She smothered the sob in her throat and chose the plainer navy dress with the bit of lace trim at the throat and sleeves. Surely this one would be quite acceptable, even proper.

She dressed in the new undergarments, and the long stockings, put on the new shoes and slipped the dress over her head. She'd wear the lighter bonnet and her new shawl. It wasn't cold enough to be needing the heavy coat.

Carefully she brushed out her curly hair and then decided to pin it up in a proper fashion. She had been dreadfully neglectful of it lately, she knew. It took her several minutes to arrange it to meet her approval, and just as she finished she heard Clark call to see if they were ready.

Missie went bursting from the room to meet her pa and was informed that she looked like a "real little lady an' her pa was right proud of her."

Marty followed, refusing to meet Clark's eyes. She didn't want to read anything there, whether real or imagined. She noticed as he helped her up to the seat of the wagon that he had changed from his work clothes and looked rather fine himself. As they travelled to the Grahams, she gave her full attention to the young Missie and the cool fall day.

The day passed quickly at the Grahams. Marty helped Ma and the girls get the dinner on. This time Marty was aware of what she ate and found Ma to be a very good cook, a fact which was no surprise to her. After the dinner the men left for the sunny side of the porch so that they could man-talk.

Young Jason Stern put in an appearance, much to the blushing of Sally Anne. The two went for a walk, always in full sight of the house.

The ladies made quick work of the dishes and then Ma and Marty sat down for a chat. It was good just to sit and talk with Ma. Marty didn't mind her idle hands half so much with such pleasant company. After discussing the general women's topics, Marty took advantage of the fact that the rest were outdoors at various activities and the two young ones put down for a nap, to broach a subject that had been stirring within her.

"Ma," she ventured, "could ya tell me 'bout Ellen? Seems thet I should be knowin' somethin' 'bout her, takin' over her house an' her baby."

Marty made no reference to "her man," Ma noticed, but made no comment on it. Marty then told Ma about the sewing machine and Clark's reaction to it.

Ma sighed deeply and seemed to look off into space for a moment. When she spoke her voice was a might shaky.

"Don't hardly know what words to be a tellin' it with," Ma said. "Ellen was young an' right pretty, too. Darker than you, she be, an' taller too. She was a merry and chattery sort. Loved everythin' an' everybody, seemed to me. She adored Clark an' he 'peared to think her somethin' pretty special, too.

"When Missie was born, ya should have see'd the two of 'em." Ma shook her head and smiled gently. "Never see'd two people so excited—like a couple of kids they were. I delivered Missie. Fact is, I've delivered most babies here 'bout, but never did I see anyone else git quite thet excited over a newborn, welcome as they be.

"Well, Ellen, she was soon up an' about an' fussin' over thet new baby. She thought she was jest beautiful, an' Missie be right pretty, too. Anyway the months went by. Clark an' Ellen was a doin' real good. Clark's a hard worker an' thet's what farmin' is all about. Ya git what yer willin' to pay fer in sweat an' achin' back. Well, things was a goin' real good when one day last August Clark came ridin' into the yard. He was real excited like an' I knew thet somethin' was wrong. 'Ma,' he says, 'can ya come quick? Ellen is in awful pain.' Thet's what he says. I can hear him yet.

"So I went, yellin' to the girls what to do while I be gone. Ellen was in pain all right, tossing an' rollin' on the bed, holdin' herself an' groanin'. She refused to cry out 'cause she didn't want Missie to hear her. So she jest bit her lip till she had it a bleedin'.

"Wasn't much thet I could do but try to keep her face cooled. There was no doctor to go fer, an' we jest watched, hurtin' all over thet we couldn't do anythin' fer her. Clark was torn between stayin' with Ellen an' carin' fer Missie. I never been so sorry fer a man.

"Well, the night dragged by an' finally 'bout four in the mornin' she stopped thrashin' so. I breathed a prayer of relief, but it wasn't to be fer long.

"She kept gettin' hotter an' hotter an' more an' more listless. I bathed her in cool water over an' over again, but it were no use."

Ma stopped, waited for a moment, then took a deep breath and went on.

"Thet evenin' we lost her, an Clark—" she stopped again.

She brushed a tear away and stood up. "But thet be in the past, child, an' no use goin' over it all agin. Anyway, ya be there now to care fer Missie an' thet's what Clark be a needin'. Was awful hard fer him to do all his fall work totin' thet little one round on his back. I said I'd keep her on here, but I reckon Clark wanted her to know thet she be his an' somethin' special, not jest one of a brood. Besides he never did want to be beholden to anybody. There was a childless woman in town who would have gladly took her, but Clark would have none of it. Said she would have growed up so spoiled she would have been unfit fer even herself to stand; that's what Clark said. Anyway, Clark's prayers seem to be gittin' answered and Missie has you now an' a right good mama ya be a makin' too—sewin' thet sweet little dress an' all."

She patted Marty's arm.

"Yer doin' jest fine, Marty. Jest fine."

Through the whole speech of Ma's, Marty had sat wide-eyed. The hearing of Clark's sorrow had opened afresh the pain of her own. She wanted to weep but sat dry-eyed, feeling the horror of it all. It had been a shock for her to hear that Clem was dead, but she hadn't had to sit by him for hours watching him suffer, not able to lift a hand to relieve him. She decided that she had had the easier suffering of the two.

"Oh, Clem," her heart whispered, "Clem, I'm glad thet ya didn't have to bear pain like thet."

She roused as Ma hustled up, exclaiming that time had just flown and the menfolk would be looking for coffee.

Chapter 14

Missie

The next morning at breakfast Clark informed Marty that Thursday of the week Missie would have her second birthday. Marty felt concern. She wasn't sure how Ellen would have celebrated the event. She didn't want to let Clark down, but how was she to know what the family chose to do about birthdays? She was rather silent, weighing the matter mentally for the rest of the meal. Clark sensed her mood and finally inquired.

"Somethin' be a troublin' ya?"

"No," lied Marty and remained silent for a few minutes, then decided that that would never do. If they had to share the same house, they'd just have to be frank and honest with one another, so she blurted out. "It's jest thet I don't know what ya would want planned fer Missie's birthday. Da ya have company? Have a party? Do somethin' different?" She shrugged. "I don't know."

"I see," Clark said, and she felt that he really did see. He got up and refilled their coffee cups.

"Dad-blame," thought Marty, "I missed thet second cup agin with my deep thinkin'."

Clark didn't appear to be at all bothered by it. He sat back down and creamed his coffee, pushing his plate back and pulling his cup forward as though preparing for a lengthy stay.

By this time Missie was getting restless and wanting down

from her chair. Clark lifted her down and she ran into the sitting room to find her new book. Clark continued then.

"Funny thing, but I don't rightly remember any fixed thing thet we be a doin' fer a birthday. Seems in lookin' back thet they were all a mite different somehow. Missie now, she only had one afore an' she was abit young then to pay it much mind," he hesitated. "I think though thet it would be nice to be a havin' a cake fer her. I got a doo-dad in town last Saturday while I was there. I hope it pleases her. Jest a silly little thing really, but it looks like it would tickle a little 'un. I don't think thet we be needin' company's help in celebratin'. She'll enjoy it jest as much on her own."

Marty felt relieved. That kind of a birthday celebration she felt that she could handle. She sat quietly for a moment and finally raised her eyes to Clark's and said almost imploringly. "I been thinkin'. Seems thet I don't know much 'bout Missie an' seems as tho' I should be a knowin' a sight more iffen I be goin' to raise her an' all. Ya know how young 'uns be. They like to hear their folks tell of when they did this an' when they said thet, an' how cute an' clever they was, an' quick in their ways an' all. Some day soon Missie's goin' to be wantin' to hear sech things, an' I should be able to tell her. The only thing I know 'bout her is her name."

Clark surprised her by laughing quietly. It was the first time that she had heard him laugh. She liked it, but she couldn't figure out the reason for it. He soon filled her in.

"I be thinkin' thet ya don't really know even thet," he said. "Her real name be Melissa—Melissa Ann Davis."

"Thet's a pretty name," Marty said. "I don't be goin' by my real name either. My real name be Martha, but I don't much like it. All my family an' friends called me Marty, 'cept my ma when she was mad. Then it was Martha, real loud like. Martha Lucinda—" She nearly finished it with Claridge but caught herself in time.

"But tell me 'bout Missie."

"Well, Missie be born on November third, two years ago, 'bout four o'clock in the mornin'."

Clark's face became very thoughtful as he reflected back. Marty remembered Ma telling of the great excitement that

Missie had caused. Clark went on.

"She weren't much of a bundle, seemed to me, an' she was rather red an' wrinkled, an' had a good head of dark hair. She seemed to grow fast an' change a lot right from the start, an' afore ya knowed it she was a cooin' an' smilin'. By Christmas time she was most givin' the orders round here it seemed. She was a good baby as babies go an' slept through the night by the time she was three months old. I thought I'd picked me a real winner. Then at five months she started to cut her teeth. She turned from a sweet contented, smilin' darlin' into a real bearcat. Lucky fer us, it didn't last fer too long, though at the time it seemed ferever. Anyway, she made it through. So did we, an' things quieted down agin.

"When she had her first birthday, she could already say some words. Seemed right bright for a little tyke, an' al'ays from as far back as I can remember she loved pretty things. Guess thet's why she took so to the little whatever it be thet ya sewed fer her.

"Started walkin' 'fore her first birthday an' was soon climbin' to match it. Boy, how she did git around! One day I found her on the corral fence, top rail, when she be jest a wee'un. Got up there an' couldn't git down. Hangin' on fer dear life she was.

"She was gettin' to be a right good visitor, too. A lot of company she was. Chattered all the time an' more an' more there was gettin' to be some sense to it.

"One day she came in with a flower. Thrilled to pieces with it she was. Picked it right off the rose bush. The thorns had pricked her tiny fingers an' they was a bleedin'. But she never paid them no mind at all, so determined she be to take the 'pretty' to her mama. Thet flower is pressed in her mama's Bible."

Clark stopped and sat looking at his coffee cup. Marty saw him swallow and his lips move as though he meant to go on, but no sound came.

"Ya don't need to tell me anymore," she said quietly. "I know enough to be able to tell young Missie somethin' 'bout her young days."

She searched for words and found that any that she could

bring to mind seemed inadequate, but she stumbled on.

"I know how painful it be—to remember, an' anyway when the day comes thet young Missie need hear the story of her mama—an' she should hear it, to be sure—but when thet day comes, it's her pa thet she should be a hearin' it from."

Marty rose from the table then so that Clark need not fear that he was expected to say more. Slowly he finished his coffee and she set to work getting her water ready to wash the dishes.

The day was almost crisp in its coolness, but Clark announced that he planned to see how much sod he could get turned on the land he was claiming for spring planting. Marty hoped that the weather would hold, not just so that he could finish the planned plowing but also so that he would be busy away from the house.

The days of the week went by slowly. Sometimes they went too slowly for Marty, but she was relieved that there was always work with which to fill them. What with washing, cleaning, bread-baking, and meal getting, she seemed to even have to look for time in which to do Missie's sewing. Little garments did take shape under her capable hands, however, and Missie fussed and exclaimed over each one of them.

Marty had a secret project on the go as well. Knowing of Missie's birthday had sent her mind scrambling over what she might be able to do for the little girl. She didn't have many options really, not having a cent to her name, even if she had found a way to spend it. She then thought of the beautifully colored wool that Clark had brought and the brand new knitting needles. Each night she retired to her room as soon as her day's tasks were taken care of and with Missie sleeping soundly in her crib, the knitting needles clicked hurriedly. She must work quickly to be done in time. When she finally crawled off to bed each night, she was too tired to even lie for long and ache for Clem. She thought of him, and her last wish of the night was that he could have been by her side, cuddling close in the big double bed; but even though her thoughts turned to him, her tired body demanded sleep and she felt too weary to even cry.

The days passed and Thursday dawned cold and windy.

Clark was still determined to carry on with his plowing even though Marty feared that he would surely take a chill by so doing. He paid no mind to her and went anyway. She wondered secretly if he wished to be away from the house as much as she wanted him to be.

After dinner was over and Missie had been put down for her nap, Marty went to work on the birthday cake. She felt much more confident now, having practiced using Ma's recipes to a fair extent. Carefully she watched her fire on this day. It would not do to have it too hot nor to let it die out as she so often did.

She sighed with relief when Missie's cake was lifted from the oven, appearing to be all that she had hoped for.

The wind was colder now and Marty found herself worrying even more about Clark. What in the world would she ever do if he took sick and needed nursing? Dad-burn man! He shouldn't be taking such chances. She'd keep the coffee pot on so that whenever he decided to come in she'd have a hot cup waiting. She'd do almost anything, she figured, to keep him on his feet and walking. Why, if he went down sick, she wouldn't know where to even start on the chores. She'd never even set foot in the barn, she realized. Some women folk had to do the milking all of the time, and for that matter, some did the slopping of the hogs, too. Clark hadn't even turned the feeding of the chickens over to her. Maybe he had expected it and she just hadn't done so. She had been so mixed up and confused when she came to this place that she hadn't even given it a thought. Well, she'd ask. Maybe tomorrow at breakfast, if the time seemed right. She was more than willing to do her rightful share.

She heard the team coming and cast an anxious glance out the window.

"He be lookin' cold all right." She pushed the coffee pot forward on the stove.

When Clark came in he stood for a few moments holding his big hands over the kitchen stove, as if trying to scoop up handfuls of the heat to warm his chilled body.

Marty poured his cup of coffee and went for some cream.

She decided to also bring some muffins and honey in case he wanted a bit to go with the hot drink.

He watched her from the stove and said nothing until she had set it by his place at the table.

"Won't ya be a joinin' me?" he asked; then, "I hate to be a drinkin' coffee all alone."

Marty looked up in surprise but answered evenly.

"Ya be the one thet be a needin' it. Ya be a chillin' yerself fer sure workin' out in thet wretched wind an' all. Lucky ya be iffen ya don't be a puttin' yerself down over it. Come, ya'd better be drinkin' this while it be hot."

It was mild scolding but something in it seemed to tickle Clark. He smiled to himself as he crossed to the table. Women—honestly, one would think a man was made of sugar frosting the way that they could carry on. He hid his smile and answered good naturedly. "I may be the one a needin' it, but I doubt thet a few minutes at the table an' off yer feet be a hurtin' ya much either. Ya fuss too much, I be a thinkin'."

"No," Marty said solemnly. "No, I don't fuss too much. I jest find thet workin' sure beats moanin', thet's all. But as ya say, a cup of coffee might be right good. I do declare, hearin' thet wind howl makes my blood chill, even though it be warm in here."

So saying, she poured herself a cup of coffee and joined him at the table.

After their coffee, Clark said that he had come home early from the plowing because he thought that a storm might be on the way and he wanted to have the rest of the garden things in the root cellar before it struck. So saying, he left the house to go to work.

Marty turned to Missie's now cooled cake. She wanted it to look 'special' for the little girl so used all of her ingenuity and material available for that purpose. When she was finally done she looked at it critically. It wasn't great, she decided, but it would have to do. She placed it in the cupboard behind closed doors to await the proper moment for its appearance. She then set to work on plans for a little something extra for supper. Missie's call interrupted her at this point and she went in for the little girl.

"Hi there, Missie. Come to Mama," she said.

She had said the words before and hadn't liked them, so she had not referred to herself as such since. As she spoke them now they didn't seem nearly so out of place, though they still seemed strange to her.

She lifted the wee one up, noticing as she did so that her own little one was demanding more room. She was glad that she had put plenty of fullness in the new dresses that she had made. Already she was needing some of it.

Missie ran to get her shoes and Marty carried child and shoes to the kitchen where she put them on. Already it was chilly in the bedroom. She dreaded the thought of the cold winter ahead. How glad she was not to be in the covered wagon. The very thought made her shiver.

She gave Missie a mug of milk and half of a muffin and went back to preparing the evening meal.

Clark finished up the work in the garden and did the evening chores a bit earlier than usual. Marty sensed in him an excitement that he had not shown before. She knew that he must have dreaded the arrival of his little girl's birthday without Ellen there to share it, but as the event drew near he wanted to make the most of it for Missie's sake.

After they had finished their supper Marty went to the cupboard for the cake. Missie's eyes opened wide in wonder, but she did not understand its meaning.

"Pretty, pretty!" she cried over and over.

"It's Missie's birthday cake," Clark explained.

"Missie is having a birthday. Missie was one year old," indicating one upright finger; "now Missie is two years old." Another finger joined the first.

"See, Missie, two years old. Here Missie, let me help ya."

He took the small hand in his big one and helped Missie hold upright two fingers.

"See, Missie, ya be two years old."

"Two—old," Missie repeated.

"Thet's right," said her pa, well pleased. "Two years old, an' now we'll have some of Missie's birthday cake."

Marty cut the cake and was surprised at how good it really was. As she tasted it she thought of her first effort with the biscuits. Now thankfully, with practice and Ma's recipes, she could turn out things that she need not be ashamed of. Three weeks had made quite a difference.

When they had finished their cake, Clark having asked for and received a second piece, Marty was about to wash the supper dishes, but Clark suggested that they first see what Missie thought of the gift he had purchased. She was only too happy to agree, as she was curious to see what would be the child's reaction.

Clark came in from the shed with a small box; then lifting Missie out of her chair, he presented it to her.

"Fer Missie's birthday," Clark said.

Missie turned and looked at the cake, as though wondering if she was to put the birthday—meaning cake—in the small box.

"Look, Missie," Clark said, "look here in the box. This is fer Missie on her birthday."

He helped the child lift the top lid and Missie stared in wonderment at the item in the box. Clark lifted it out, wound it firmly and placed it on the floor. When he released it, it began to spin, whirling out in many colors of red, blue, yellow, violet—too many to really name.

Missie clasped her hands together excitedly, too awestruck to say anything.

When it stopped whirling she pushed it toward Clark, saying, "Do it 'gain." Clark did.

Marty watched for some time before she turned to the dishes, and then suddenly she remembered her own gift. It certainly wasn't anything as grand as Clark's, she mused, as she carried it from the bedroom. Maybe Missie wouldn't care for it at all. Well, she'd done what she could with what she had. So be it.

"Missie," she said as she entered the kitchen, "I have somethin' fer ya, too," and she held out her gift.

Clark's eyes widened.

"Well, I be," he muttered. "Missie, jest look what yer mama done made ya."

Marty knelt in front of the little girl and carefully fitted round her shoulders the small shawl that she had labored over. It was done in a soft blue with pink rosebuds embroidered on it. Tassles lined the edge and they seemed to especially intrigue the little girl whose hands kept feeling them.

"Oh," said Missie. "Oh, Mama."

It was the first time that she had called her Mama, and Marty found herself swallowing a big lump in her throat. She tried to hide her feelings by adjusting the shawl to hang right.

Suddenly she was aware that Clark was looking at her, and there was a puzzled look on his face. Marty glanced down self-consciously and in so doing saw with horror the reason for the look. In kneeling before the child she had knelt on her skirt, pinning it down firmly, its tightness outlining her growing body, revealing it noticeably. Flushing, she clambered to her feet.

"Now I've gone an' done it," she thought. Well, she couldn't have gone on hiding it forever anyway. Besides, why should she feel any shame? It was Clem's baby, conceived in wedlock and love. She couldn't help that he was no longer here to share the bornin' of it. Still, she didn't know why, but she just wished that this man who had taken her in didn't have to know about it until it was there, arrived and already growing. Well, there was no use to go frettin' about it. He knew now and there was nothin' that she could be a doin' about it.

She turned to the dishes and Clark went back to playing with Missie.

Chapter 15

Disclosed Secret

Next morning the sky was dark-scowling. The wind still blew from the north, telling the world that it was now in charge. The horses huddled, backs to the storm, and the cows gathered in the shelter of the barn trying to escape the chill of the gale. Very few chickens appeared outside of the coop, and those that did soon dashed back to the warmth of the building. As Marty noted them, she remembered her resolve to speak to Clark about assuming the care of them.

"Dad-burn," she exclaimed, "I sure did pick me a grand time to be a startin'."

Clark's prayer at breakfast that morning included a thanks to the Almighty for the warm shelter that was theirs, both for man and beast, and for the fact that they need not fear the coldness of the winter, due to the mercies of their great God. "An' to the hard work of the man hisself," added Marty mentally. However, she did acknowledge the truth of the prayer. It was comforting to know that they were prepared for the cold weather ahead.

Marty was just getting around again to wondering what on earth she would do with Clark around the house all day, when he took her completely off guard.

"I be a leavin' fer town right away," he said. "Is there anythin' thet ya be a needin'?"

"But it's only Friday," Marty responded.

"Yes'm, I know thet, but I have some business there thet I'd like to be a seein' to right away like, an' if a storm comes up we might jest have to sit tight a spell."

Marty couldn't help but feel that the idea was a very foolish one. This time he'd take a chill for sure. He'd managed to somehow sneak past his last tempting of fate without appearing any the worse for it, but surely he couldn't be that lucky again. But who was she to argue, and with a man? If they made up their minds, there just wasn't much that a body could do about it. She left the table and checked out her list to see if anything else needed to be added.

Clark sat mulling over his coffee, then finally spoke. "Me bein' a man I didn't notice what I s'pose a woman would have see'd long ago. I had me no idea thet ya was expectin' a young 'un."

Marty did not look away from her list. She did not want to meet his eyes.

"I'm right sorry thet I didn't know. I might have saved ya some hard things. From now on ya'll do no more totin' of them heavy water pails. When ya be needin' extra water fer washin' an' sech, ya be a lettin' me know."

How silly, thought Marty. If this baby gonna be harmed by a totin' water, the damage be done long ago.

Still she said nothing and Clark went on. "We be blessed with lots of good fresh milk. I hope ya be a takin' advantage of it. If there be anythin' ya need or anythin' I can do, I'd be obliged if ya let me know."

He paused, then went on. "Seein' as how I be goin' to town today anyhow, I figured as how maybe Missus McDonald would fix up a bundle of sewing pieces thet ya be a needin' to sew baby things. If there be anythin' in particular thet ya be settin' yer mind on, then try to describe it fer her on the list."

Marty stood tongue-tied. She hadn't gotten around to worrying yet how she would clothe the new young one. It still seemed so very far off in the future, but Clark was right. She must start sewing or she'd never be ready. Now near panic seized her.

"Thank ya," she answered Clark. "I'm sure Missus

McDonald be knowin' better'n me what I be needin'," and she handed him the completed list.

She looked out of the window, still anxious about the weather. Storms came suddenly sometimes, she was told, and she hated to see Clark set out when there was a chance that one was on the way. He seemed to read her thoughts.

"Plenty of time to git to town an' back," he said. "Iffen a storm should catch me, there be plenty of neighbors livin' between here an' town, an' I'd be able to take shelter with one of them if I be a needin' to."

"But, but, what 'bout the chores?" Marty stammered. "I don't even know what to do or where to find the feed, or nuthin'."

Clark swung around to face her and it was clear from the look on his face that he had not considered the question of her with the chores.

"Iffen a storm be a comin' an' I have to shelter an' don't make it home, ya don't leave this house. Do ya hear?"

Marty heard, loud and clear.

"Don't ya dare worry ya none 'bout the hens or the hogs or even the milk cows. Nuthin'—I mean nuthin'—out there be so important thet I want ya out 'there a carin' fer it."

"So that's the way it be," thought Marty. "Well, he needn't be so riled up 'bout it."

It was the closest to upset that she had ever seen Clark, and she couldn't help but feel surprise. He turned from her, buttoned his heavy jacket and reached for his mitts. He hesitated. "Might be a fine day to be a piecin' a quilt. The little feller will be a needin' a warm un."

"Yeah," Marty thought, "he most likely will."

"I'll be back fer chore time," Clark said as she moved to go out the door; then he paused a moment and said quietly, "I be right glad thet ya'll have a little 'un to remember 'im by"— and he was gone.

Chapter 16

Thoughtful and Carin'

Clark returned in time for the chores, much to Marty's relief. By then the snow was falling, swirling around angrily as it came. Clark went right on down to the barn to care for Dan and Charlie.

"He be settin' more stock on them horses then on his own self," Marty, watching from the kitchen window, murmured to herself.

She moved to the stove and pushed the coffee that she had ready, closer to the center of the fire box so that it would be sure to be hot.

Missie had been playing on the floor, but when she heard Ole Bob's joyous bark of welcome she jumped up, eyes shining.

"Daddy comin'," she said excitedly.

Marty smiled at the fact that Missie often said daddy even though Clark referred to himself as pa. Ellen must have preferred "daddy," Marty decided. Well, then for Ellen's sake she would go on talking about daddy to her, too.

Clark was soon in, arms full of bundles and face red from the cold wind. At the sight of her pa, Missie danced a wild jig.

"Daddy here—Daddy here. Hi, Pa."

Clark called out to her and when he had rid himself of his parcels, swung the little girl up into his arms where she exclaimed over his cold face as she patted his cheeks.

"Best ya be a warmin' up a bit 'fore ya start the chores,"
Marty told him as she poured a cup of coffee.

"Sounds like a right good idea," he responded, taking off
his heavy coat and hanging it by the fire to let it warm until he
needed it again. He stood for a moment warming his hands
and then crossed to the table. Marty creamed the coffee and
placed it before him.

"Thet there fair-sized bundle be yourn," Clark said. "Missus McDonald was right excited bout fixin' it up. Think she
was a mite confused. Seemed to think it was my young 'un. It
bein' none of her business, I didn't bother none to set her
straight."

He swallowed a few more gulps of hot coffee. Marty's
thoughts whirled.

"His young 'un. How could it be his young 'un, us not even
bein' true man an' wife? Course Missus McDonald wouldn't
be a knowin' thet." She felt shame coloring her face.

Clark went on. "I got a thinkin' later, though, thet maybe I
should have said somethin' so I went back. 'Missus McDonald,' I sez, 'true, my Missus be havin' a young 'un and true I'll
be a treatin' 'im as one of mine, but also true thet his pa be her
first husband an' thet bein' important to her, I wouldn't want
folks gettin' things mixed up like.' "

Clark finished his coffee.

"Well, I best be gettin'."

Clark hurried into his coat and was gone before Marty had
time to catch her breath.

He understood. He'd gone back to the store to set Mrs. Mc-
Donald straight because he knew, as did everyone there about,
that her tongue was the busiest part of her anatomy. Give her
a day or two of fair weather and everyone in the area would
know of the coming baby. Yet Clark understood that it was
important to her that he be known as Clem's baby. Her mind
continued to try to sort out this man as she began to put away
the supplies that he had purchased.

When she turned excitedly to her bundle, she decided to
take it in on her bed to open it. It was cold in the bedroom now
and she shivered, partly from anticipation, she was sure, as
she unwrapped the brown store paper.

Mrs. McDonald had gone all out. Marty gasped as she looked at the beautiful materials. Surely a young 'un didn't need that many baby things. Her cheeks flushed at the thought of the days and evenings ahead when she could sit and work on the small garments. She wished that she had someone to share it with and was tempted to pour it all out to Missie. No, she'd best wait awhile for that. The remaining months would seem far too long for a two-year-old. Oh, if only Clem were here to share it with her. A hot tear trickled down Marty's cheek. She brushed it away with the back of her hand. If only it were that easy to get rid of the pain in her heart!

When Clark came in to supper, he was noticeably shivering in spite of his heavy coat. He remarked that he couldn't believe how much the temperature had dropped in a few short hours. The wind had a great deal to do with it.

Before he sat down to the table he lit a fire in the fireplace in the sitting room.

"Guess it's time," he observed, "to be havin' more heat than jest the cook stove."

When he prayed that night he asked his God to be with "people less blessed than we," and Marty was reminded of her covered wagon with the broken wheel and she shivered to think of what it would be like to be huddled in it now, trying to keep warm under their scant blankets.

After the meal Clark moved to the sitting room to check and replenish the fire, and Missie moved her few toys to the rug in front of it.

Marty did the dishes, feeling warm and protected in spite of herself; for how else could one feel in a snug cabin, while the wind screamed around you unable to get in?

The evening was still young and Marty was anxious to get started on her sewing, but she realized how cold her room would be. She was still trying to find some answer to her problem as she emptied her dishpan and replaced it on its peg, when Clark spoke.

"It'll be right cold in yer room from now on. Do ya be a wantin' yer machine moved out to the sittin' room? There be plenty of room there fer it."

Marty looked directly at him as she answered slowly, "Do

ya mind seein' it a sittin' there?"

He answered her in honesty, knowing that she understood. "S'pose I do some. But it's not as hard now as it was at first sight of it, an' twould be only foolhardy not to put it where it can be of use. I'll git used to it," and so saying he went to do as he had suggested.

"Yes," Marty thought to herself. She was discovering that this man would do the right thing even if it did hurt him.

She felt a little selfish about her anticipation of being able to do her sewing in the warm room. If things had to be as they were, she certainly could have done worse. She still ached for her Clem. She wished him back even if it would have meant having as little as they had. Still she would be unfair if she refused to see the goodness in this man whose name she had taken and whose home she shared. That he was a real worker and a good provider was apparent, but she was discovering other things about him, too—things like thoughtfulness and caring. Certainly she couldn't fault him in his demands on her. She was only to be Missie's mama. He hadn't even complained about her terrible cooking. No, she decided, even though she still didn't like her situation, she certainly could have done worse.

She set her mind on her sewing. She would give Missie a bit more playing time before she tucked her in.

Clark had settled himself with one of his new books. Marty thankfully picked up a pattern that Mrs. McDonald had included. She had never sewed for one so small before and would have been hard put to know how to cut the material without the pattern. Her hands fairly shook with excitement. She'd do the cutting on the kitchen table where she had more room.

Chapter 17

Mysterious Absence

The days of November slipped slowly by. The storms came and went. Snow lay heavy on the fields and big drifts rose around sheltered spots where the wind had shifted the snow. Some days the wind ceased blowing and the sun shone, but always the temperature stayed below freezing. Activity on the small homestead did not cease because of the weather. There was still much to do. On the fairer days Clark spent his time with Dan and Charlie up in the wooded back country gathering logs for their wood supply for the coming year.

On the more miserable days there was more time spent in choring to try to ease the animals through the storms with as little discomfort as possible.

Marty, too, kept busy. Caring for Missie, keeping the house, baking bread, washing, mending, ironing—the list seemed endless to her, yet she was thankful to have each of the long days filled with things that needed to be done.

In the evenings she went gladly to her sewing, making each stitch on the tiny garments with tender care. She had laid aside the quilt she had begun. It could wait. She wanted to busy herself with preparations for the baby.

She had noticed that Clark had referred to it as "he" also. It could surprise them both and be a girl, she knew, but stubbornly refused to think of it other than as a male child.

She'd already decided on his name—Claridge Luke. Claridge after his pa, and Luke after hers. How proud her pa would be to know that he had a grandson bearing his name. But that would have to wait for the first wagon train going east, when she'd pack up her son and the young Missie and be heading back home.

It was beginning to bother her about taking Missie. She saw the great love that Clark had for his little girl, and she wondered when the time came if he'd really be able to let her go. Marty was getting awfully attached to Missie herself. Referring to herself as Mama came easy now. Indeed, sneaking up quite unawares was the feeling that she was just that. Each day she enjoyed the young child's company more, laughing at her silly antics, marvelling at her new words, and even sharing some of the same with Clark when he came home at nights.

If she had stopped to think about it, she would have realized that Missie was becoming very much a part of her life. She could hardly wait for the new year, the time she had decided that she would tell her secret to the little girl. She was sure that the child would share her anticipation of the new baby. But Marty went on day by day, not making any attempt to stop to think or to analyze her gradually changing feelings. It was enough just to tick the slow days off, discarding them casually at day's end, like something that had served its purpose merely by coming and going; for indeed, Marty was still marking time.

As November drew to a close, Marty suddenly realized that it seemed Clark had made an unusual number of trips into town, especially for that time of the year. It wasn't as though they had need of supplies. Indeed, he sometimes returned with very few purchases, and sometimes he even used the saddle horse rather than the team. Marty hadn't even thought to wonder about it at first, but the morning's breakfast conversation had her puzzled. Clark had announced casually enough that he would be gone for three or four days. There appeared to be a bit of a break in the weather, so he had decided that now was the time to make his planned trip to a much larger center than their small town. Young Tom Graham would be coming in the evening and staying the night to look after the evening and morning chores. If the weather should turn sour, she could ask him to stay on through the day as well. If she was in need of anything, she could send word with Tom to the Grahams.

His words had puzzled Marty. He had made an unusual number of trips, but really it was none of her business. Probably he was looking for new machinery to till the land, or better seed, or a place to sell his hogs. Anyway it was his business, so why should she worry herself about it. Young Tom would be over. There was nothing to fret about.

Still in all, as Clark gave Missie a good-bye hug and admonished her to be a good, big girl for her mama, Marty couldn't help but feel a bit of uneasiness.

"I'll be back Saturday night in time fer chores," he promised and went out for Dan and Charlie. As Marty watched him leave the yard, she noticed that the crate was in the wagon box and a couple of hogs were having a ride to town. What had he said?

"If we be a needin' more cash, we can al'ays sell a hog."

This too puzzled Marty. Truly he must be shopping for another plow or more seed, she decided. Still, on the other hand, she had cost him a powerful lot of extra money, what with the winter clothing for herself, the wool for knitting and the pieces for quilting, and then to top it off, the things for the baby. Yes, she had cost him an awful lot of money.

Marty fretted over it a bit, something that she usually kept herself from doing. Finally she pushed it aside with real effort.

"No use a takin' on so. Guess I'm jest a mite off my feed or somethin' to be a stewin' 'bout it so. Wisht I could have me a good visit with Ma. Thet'd set things to right. By the time Clark gits back it'll be December already."

Time was moving on, no matter how slow it seemed at times, and hadn't Ma said that it was time that healed? She was glad to see the days go by. She hoped that they would go quickly while Clark was away.

When Clark returned on Saturday, Marty was more relieved than she would admit to see the team coming. She didn't know why she should be. Young Tom had done a fine job of the chores she was sure, and she hadn't at all minded his company in the evenings. After supper he played with Missie or read her book to her over and over. He was proud of the fact that he had learned his letters and knew how to read, as did each one of Ma's children, and he loved to show off to Missie, and, Marty smiled, to her as well, she wagered. By now Missie could repeat many of the lines of her book herself as she had heard them so often, but that had no effect at all on her love to hear it again.

They had gotten along just fine while Clark was away, so that had no bearing on her sense of relief to see him home. Perhaps deep down within her was the memory of a casual good-bye to Clem and a later discovery that it had been the last.

Missie was overjoyed at the sight of her daddy and began a dance as soon as she spotted him from her chair at the window.

Marty noticed that the crate was now empty, but she could see no evidence of a purchase made from the proceeds. Only a few small packages sat on the seat beside Clark. Dan and Charlie looked weary, she thought, as she watched them plod toward the barn. Their steps hastened some, as they drew near, in their eagerness to reach warm stalls and a full manger.

Clark looked tired, too, she decided, as she watched him leap down and begin to unhitch the team. He wasn't moving with the same lightness that usually accompanied his step.

"Well, he's here now an' he'll be a wantin' some hot coffee."

This fact presented no problem, for Marty had the coffee boiled and on hand. Now she could stop her pacing to the window, looking down the road for the team, though she had been quite unaware that she had been doing so.

Life, she hoped, would continue on now in its usual way. It wasn't what she had wanted from life, but at least it had taken on a pattern now familiar to her, and there was a certain amount of comfort even in the familiar.

Clark came in with his few articles of groceries and she welcomed him with a cup of coffee.

Chapter 18

Christmas Preparations

"Our God," Clark prayed in his morning prayer, "as we be nearin' the season of yer Son's birth, make our hearts thankful thet He came, an' help us to be a lovin' our neighbor with a love like He showed us."

"He's talkin' 'bout Christmas," Marty thought with a sudden awareness of the season. "Oh, my, it be only two weeks away an' I haven't even been a thinkin' on it."

Her mind went plunging from thought to thought so that again she missed the rest of the prayer and sat with eyes still closed after the 'Amen' until Missie pulled at her sleeve, wanting her breakfast.

She lifted a flushed face and hurriedly fixed Missie's porridge for her, blowing on it to cool it some before giving it to the child.

"Ya know," she ventured a little later, "I had fergot all 'bout how close Christmas be."

Clark looked up from his eating.

"I know Christmas be a mite hard to be a thinkin' on this year. Iffen it be too hard fer ya, we can most ferget the day, 'cept fer the reading of the Story an' maybe a sock fer young Missie."

Marty thought for a few minutes.

"No," she finally answered. "Thet wouldn't be right. Missie needs her Christmas—a proper one like, an' I reckon it may do us good, too. We can't stay back there in the past nursin' our sorrow—not for her sake, nor fer our own. Christmas, seems to me, be a right good time to lay aside hurtin' an' look fer somethin' healin'.''

Clark's eyes widened. Seemed that he had never heard a better sermon from any visiting preacher than the one he'd just heard from Marty. When he recovered enough to speak in his normal manner, he responded. "Ya be right of course. So what ya be plannin'?"

"Well—" Marty turned it over in her mind trying to recall exactly what had happened at her home to prepare for Christmas. Of course there hadn't been the reading of the scripture story, but they could add that; and there had been a good supply of corn likker, which they could do without. Otherwise, there must be several things that she could do the way her mother had. This would be her first Christmas away from home—the first Christmas for her to make for others, rather than have others make for her. The thought made her feel both edgy and excited.

"Well," she repeated again. "I'll git me to doin' some Christmas bakin'. Maybe Ma has some special recipes she'll share. Then we'll have a tree fer Missie. Christmas Eve we'll put it up after she be tucked in, an' we'll string pop-corn an' make some colored chains, an' have a few candles fer the windows, an' we'll kill a couple of the finest roosters, an' I'll find me somethin' to be a makin' fer Missie—"

The excitement showing in her eyes and voice was infectious. Clark, too, found himself slowly caught up in the anticipation of the coming Christmas.

"Roosters nuthin'." he said. "I'll go myself an' buy us a turkey from the Vickers. Missus Vickers raises some first-rate 'uns. Maybe there be somethin' we can be a makin' fer Missie together. I'll ride over to Ma's today an' git the recipes, or better still, it looks like a decent day. Ya be wantin' me to hitch ole Dan an' Charlie so ya can be a goin' yerself?"

"Oh, could I?" Marty's voice was almost a plea. "I'd love to see Ma fer a chat iffen yer sure it be all right."

So it was decided that Marty would go to the Grahams, but Clark added another dimension to the plan. If it was okay with her, he'd drive her to Ma's and then he and Missie would go on to the Vickers and get the turkey. That way they'd be sure to have it when the big day arrived. Missie could do with some fresh air, too.

Marty hurried through the dishes as Clark went to get the team. She bundled Missie up snuggly and slipped into her long coat. It was the first time that she had worn it, and she thought, looking at herself with a grin, perhaps the last for a while. Two of the buttons refused to meet their matching buttonholes. She sighed. "Well," she decided, taking her shawl, "guess I'll jest have to cover up the rest a' me with this."

The day spent with Ma was a real treat. They poured over Ma's recipes, Marty choosing so many that she'd never get them all baked and would be forced to choose some from among the many at a later date. She also wrote down careful instructions on how to stuff and roast the turkey, it being her first attempt at such. They shared plans and discussed possibilities for the holiday ahead. Marty felt a stirring of new interest within her at the anticipation of it. For too long she had felt that the young life she carried was the only living part of her. Now for the first time in months she began to feel alive again.

The day went all too quickly. Before she knew it she heard the team approaching. Clark was called in for a cup of coffee before setting off for home, and he came in carrying a rosy-faced Missie, excited by her ride and eager to tell everyone of the 'gobble-gobble' they had in the wagon for 'Christ'as'.

Marty could hear the live turkey protesting his leave of the flock. He would be placed in the hen's coop and generously given cracked corn and other fattening things until a few days before Christmas.

Missie romped with young Lou while the grown-ups had their coffee, too excited to even finish her glass of milk.

On the way home Marty voiced a thought that had gradually been taking shape within her. She was a bit hesitant and hardly knew how to express it, lest it be denied her.

"Do ya spose—I mean, would ya' all mind iffen we had the Grahams come fer Christmas dinner?"

"All of 'em?" It was said in shock.

"Course all of 'em. I know there be thirteen of 'em an' three of us; thet makes sixteen. The kitchen table, stretched out like, will hold eight. Thet's the four grown-ups an' the four youngest of the Grahams. Missie'll be in her chair. Thet leaves seven Graham young 'uns. We'll fix 'em a place in the sittin' room an' Laura an' Sally Anne can look to 'em."

She would have babbled on but Clark, with a laugh and an upright hand, stopped her.

"Whoa." Then he went on. "I see ya got it all sorted out. Did ya speak with Ma on it?"

"Course not," said Marty sounding almost insulted. "I wouldn't be a doin' thet afore I checked with you."

He looked sideways at her, and his voice took on a serious note. "I don't know." He hesitated. "Seems to me it be a pretty big order, gettin' on a Christmas dinner fer sixteen, an' servin' it in our small quarters, an' ya bein' the way ya are an' all."

Marty knew that she must fight for it, if it was to be. She scoffed at his protest.

"Pawsh! There be nuthin' wrong with the way I be. I feel as pert now as I ever did. As to fixin' the dinner, I'll have as much of thet done ahead as I can, afore the house packs jam tight. Then t'won't be sech a problem. When they gits there Ma and the girls will give a hand—an' with the dishes too. Oh, my—"

She stopped and fairly squealed. "The dishes! Clark, do we have enough dishes to set so many?"

"I don't know, but iffen ya don't, Ma'll bring some of hers along."

"Good!"

She smiled to herself. He had as good as said that they could come. She had sort of swung him off the track by diverting his attention to the dishes. She felt a bit guilty, but not enough to be bothered by it. "It be settled then," she ventured, and it was more a statement than a question.

Chapter 19

Snowbound

Clark went back to spending his days in the hills felling trees, and Marty went to work in her kitchen. She pored over the recipes and after finally making her choices, spent day after day turning out tempting goodies. Baked goods began to stock up almost alarmingly and she was having a hard time finding a place to put them.

Missie sampled and approved, preferring the gingerbread boys that Marty had made especially for the children.

In the evenings she and Clark worked on a doll house for Missie. Clark had constructed a simple two-room structure and was busy making wooden chairs, tables and beds. Marty's part was to put in small curtains, rugs and blankets. "Those things a woman usually be a makin'," Clark said. She had found it fun helping with the project, watching it take shape. As they worked they got new inspiration. The kitchen had a small cupboard with doors that really opened, a table, two chairs and a bench. This was Clark's work. Marty had put up little kitchen curtains, added a couple of bright rugs on the floor and put small cushions on the chairs.

The sitting-bedroom had a small bed complete with blankets and pillows, a tiny cradle, two chairs, a foot stool and a trunk with a lid that lifted. Marty still had to fix the blanket and pillow for the cradle and the curtains for this room. Clark was working on a stove for the kitchen.

"Wouldn't be much of a kitchen without a stove," he reasoned.

Marty was pleased with their effort and relieved that they should easily have it finished in time for Missie's Christmas.

Clark had made a couple more trips into town, stopping the first time to invite the Grahams to Christmas dinner. He seemed to feel that these trips were so important, yet as far as Marty could see, he had nothing to show for them when he returned. She shrugged it off.

The last time he had gone he had brought back some special spices for her baking and a few trinkets for Missie.

"She be a needin' somethin' fer her Christmas sock," he said, as he handed them into Marty's care.

Marty reviewed all of this in her thinking as she laid cookies out to cool.

"Would Clark be expecting a gift from her?" Marty wondered. She supposed not. It would have been nice to have some little thing for him, but she had no money for purchases and no way of buying anything if she did have. And what could one sew for a man?

As she worked she remembered the piece of soft blue-gray wool that still lay in her sewing basket. After she finished the cookies she'd take a look at it and see if it were possible to make a man's scarf out of the material.

When she later checked the material, she decided that it was quite possible, and knowing that Clark wouldn't be in from cutting trees until chore time, she set to work. She finished the stitching, finding it necessary to do a bit of piecing, and then tucked it away. Tomorrow while Clark was away she would hand embroider his initials on it.

Christmas would soon be here. She wondered if the day itself would be half as exciting as the preparations for it had been.

Day three—only three days to go now. They had finished their gift for Missie the night before and complimented each other on the outcome. Now breakfast was over and Clark had gone back to cutting wood. Marty had asked him to keep an eye open for nice pine branches bearing cones so that she might form a few wreaths. He said that he would see what he could do.

He would work in the morning in the hills and in the afternoon he would kill the gobbler, who at the present was going without his breakfast. Marty hurried through her morning tasks, then took up the scarf for Clark. Carefully she stitched a bold C. D. on it, and had it tucked away in her drawer before Clark arrived for dinner.

Day two—two days until Christmas, but the day was the Lord's Day, and any further preparations would have to wait. Marty conceded that perhaps a day of rest was not such a bad idea, and when Missie was tucked in for her afternoon nap, she stretched out on her own bed, with a warm blanket drawn over her. She felt weary, really weary, and the weight of the baby she carried made every task that she took on doubly hard. She closed her eyes and gave herself up to a delightful sleep.

Day one—the morrow would be Christmas. The tom was killed and hung to chill in preparation for stuffing. Marty had carefully formed her wreaths, pleased with Clark's selected branches, and tied them with her cherished store twine. She had placed one in each window and one on the door. A small tree had come from the hills with Clark and waited expectantly until the time when Missie would be tucked in bed and it would be placed in a corner of the sitting room. The corn had been popped and strung and Marty had made chains from the bits of colored paper that she had come up with. She had even made some out of the brown storewrap that had come from town.

The scarf lay completed, but as Marty looked at it a feeling of uneasiness possessed her. Somehow it didn't seem the thing to be giving a man like Clark. She wondered if she'd really have the courage to go through with it.

"Well," she said, shelving the matter, "I'll have to be a handlin' thet when the time comes, an' jest keep my mind on what I'm a doin' now."

What she was 'a doin' now' was peeling large quantities of carrots, turnips and potatoes for the morrow's meal. There would be cabbage to dice as well. The batch of bread was raising and would soon be ready for baking. The beans were soaking and would be flavored with cured ham later. Canned greens and pickles were lined up on the floor by the cupboard, waiting to be opened, and wild nuts were placed in a basket by the fireplace to be roasted over the open fire.

Mentally Marty ticked off her list. Things seemed to be going as scheduled. She looked around her at the abundance of food. Tomorrow promised to be a good day and tonight they'd have the fun of decking the tree for Missie, and hanging her sock.

Christmas Day! Marty opened her eyes earlier than usual and already her head was spinning. She must prepare the stuffing for the turkey, put the vegetables on to cook in her largest kettles, bring in plenty of the baking from the shed where it was sure to be frozen in this weather. Her mind raced on as she quickly dressed.

The room felt so cold she'd be glad to get to the warm kitchen. She crossed to check that Missie was properly covered, then quietly tiptoed from the room.

It was cold in the sitting room, too, and she hurried on to the kitchen. There was no lamp lit there so Clark was not up. She shivered as she hastened to light it and moved on to start the fire. It was so cold that her hands already felt numb. She could hear the wind whining around the cabin as she coaxed the blaze to take hold. It would be a while before the chill left the air. She moved into the sitting room to light the fire there. She must have it warm for when Missie got up.

When both fires were burning she checked the clock. Twenty minutes to six. No wonder Clark wasn't up yet. He usually rose about six-thirty in the winter months. Well, she needed every minute that she could get. She had so much to do.

She turned to the frost-covered window and scratching a small opening with her fingers, she pressed her face to the pane to look out on Christmas Day. An angry wind swirled heavily falling snow, piling drifts in seemingly mountainous proportions. She could not even see the well at times for the density of it.

Marty didn't need to be told that she was witnessing a dreaded prairie blizzard. The pain of it all began to seep in, taking possession of her. She wanted to scream out against it, to curse it away, to throw herself on her bed in a torrent of tears. Her shoulders sagged, she felt weary and defeated, but what good would it do to strike back? The storm would still rage. No one in their right mind would defy it simply for a Christmas dinner. She was licked. She felt dead again. Then suddenly a new anger took hold of her. Why? Why should the storm win?

"Go ahead," she stormed inwardly. "Go ahead and howl. We have the turkey ready to go in the oven. We have lots of food. We have our tree. We have Missie—we'll—we'll jest still have Christmas!"

She wiped her tears on her apron, squared her shoulders and turned back to add more wood to the fire. She had not noticed Clark standing there, boots in hand, watching her.

He cleared his throat and she looked up. What could he say? He knew the hurt that she was feeling. She had worked so hard for this day and now she was cheated out of it. What could he possibly say? But Marty said it for him. She stopped in front of him as he sat lacing his boots and with a smile that he could not believe and a wave of her hand toward the laden cupboard said, "My word. What we ever gonna be a doin' with all this food? We'll have to spend the whole day a eatin' on it."

She moved back to the cupboard to prepare the turkey for roasting.

"I do hope thet the Grahams haven't been caught short-fixed fer Christmas. Us a sittin' here with so few an' all this food, an' them sittin' there with so many—"

Clark sat open-mouthed. When he trusted himself to speak he said persuasively, "Ma's too smart to be took off guard like. She knows this country's mean streak. I don't think they be a wantin' at all."

Marty seemed relieved at that.

"I be right glad to hear thet," she said. "The storm had me a worryin'."

Clark sat quietly while she finished stuffing the turkey, then hurried forward when it looked oven ready.

"Best ya let me be a liftin' thet bird. He's right heavy."

Marty did not object. The turkey was in and the stove was gradually warming the kitchen. Marty put on the coffee pot and then took a chair.

"Seems the storm nearly won," she acknowledged slowly, "but it can't win unless ya let it, can it?"

Clark said nothing but his eyes told her that he understood her disappointment—and more than that, her triumph over it.

He reached out and touched her hand. When he spoke his voice was gentle. "I'm right proud of ya."

He had never touched her before except for helping her in and out of the wagon, something about it sent a warm feeling through her. Maybe it was just knowing that he understood. She hoped he hadn't noticed her reaction to his touch and in order to cover, spoke. "We'll have to cook the whole turkey, but we can freeze what we can't eat. I'll put the vegetables in smaller pots an' cook only what we be a needin'. The rest will keep fer a while in the cold pit. The bakin' "—she stopped and lifted a hand to the baking, as though it were a hopeless thing, and then she laughed. "We be eatin' thet till spring iffen we don't git some help."

"Thet's one thing thet I don't be complaining 'bout," Clark said. "Here I was a worryin' 'bout all those Graham young 'uns with their hefty appetites a comin' an' not leavin' anythin' fer me, an' now look at me, blessed with it all."

"Clark," Marty said in mocked shock, "did you go an' pray this storm?"

She'd never heard him laugh so heartily before and she joined in with him. By then the coffee was boiling and she poured two cups while he went for the cream. The kitchen was warmer now and the hot coffee washed away the last of the chill in her.

"Well," she said, getting up as quickly as her heavy burden would allow her to, "we may as well have some bakin' to go with it. Gotta git started on it sometime. What ya be fancyin'?"

Clark chose a spicy tart and Marty took a simple shortbread cookie.

They talked of the day ahead as they shared their coffee. Clark wouldn't do the chores until after Missie was up. That way he wouldn't miss her excitement. Then they would have a late breakfast and their Christmas dinner mid-afternoon. The supper meal would be the "pickin's," Clark said. That would save Marty from being over the stove all day. It sounded like a reasonable plan to her and she endorsed it wholeheartedly.

"We used to play a game when I was a kid," Clark said. "Haven't played a game fer years, but it might be fun. It was drawed out on a piece a paper or a board an' ya used pegs or buttons. While ya be busyin' about, I'll make us up one."

The clock ticked on and the snow did not cease nor the wind slacken, but it didn't matter now. It had been accepted as it was and the necessary emotional adjustments had been made.

When Missie called to get up, Clark went for her and Marty stationed herself by the sitting-room fire to watch the little girl's response. They were not disappointed. Missie was beside herself with excitement. She went from the small toys in her sock to the doll house, then to the sock, back to the doll house, exclaiming over and over the wonder of it all. Finally she stopped between the two, clasped her tiny hands together and said, "Oh, Chris'as bootiful."

Clark and Marty laughed at her. She was off again, kneeling before the doll house, handling each small item carefully as she took it out and placed it back again.

Clark finally pulled himself away to go to do the chores. The storm was still raging and he dressed warmly against it. Caring for the stock would be a heavy task on such a day, and he was glad that the animals were able to be sheltered from the wind.

Marty worried as she watched him go. The snow was so thick at times that you couldn't see the barn. She was glad that he took Ole Bob with him, as he could sense directions should the storm confuse Clark. He also left instructions with her. If he wasn't in at a set time, she was to fire the gun into the air and repeat it, if necessary, at five-minute intervals. Marty hoped that it wouldn't be necessary.

Much to Marty's relief, Clark was in before the appointed time, chilled by the wind but reporting all things in order and cared for.

She put the finishing touches on breakfast and they sat down to eat. Missie could hardly bear to leave her new toys and came only when promised that she could return to them following the meal.

They all bowed their heads and Clark prayed.

"Sometimes, Lord, we be puzzlin' bout yer ways. Thank ya, Lord, thet the storm came well afore the Grahams be a settin' out. We wouldn't want 'em caught in sech a one."

Marty hadn't thought of that but she totally agreed.

"An' Lord, thank ya fer those who share our table, an' bless this day of yourn. May it be one thet we can remember with warm feelin's even if the day be cold. Thank ya, Lord, fer this food thet ya have provided by yer goodness. Amen."

"Amen," said Missie, then she looked at her pa. "The house," she pointed, "thanks—house."

Clark looked puzzled. Marty, too, felt bewildered but tried to understand what the small child meant.

"I believe she be wantin' ya to say thanks fer her doll house," Marty ventured.

"Is thet it? Okay, Missie, we pray again. An' thank ya, Lord, fer Missie's doll house. Amen."

Missie was satisfied, and after her own 'Amen' she began to eat her breakfast.

The day went quickly. They roasted nuts at the open fire, played the game that Clark had made, which Marty won with alarming consistency, and watched Missie at her play. When she was later tucked in for an early nap, Marty got busy with the final dinner preparations. After the child awoke they would have their Christmas dinner. She wanted everything to be just right. From pancakes to a bountiful table spread with all manner of good things in just a little over two months. Marty was pleased with herself.

After they had eaten more than enough of the sumptuous meal, Clark suggested that they read the Christmas story in the sitting room while their food settled.

"Yer turnin' out to be a right fine cook," he observed, and Marty flushed at the compliment.

They moved to the sitting room and Clark took Missie on his knee and opened up the Bible. He first read of the angel appearing to the virgin girl, Mary, telling her that she had been chosen as the mother of the Christ-child. He went on to read of Joseph's and Mary's trip to Bethlehem where no room was found in the inn, so that that night the infant Jesus was born in a stable. The shepherds heard the good news from the angels and rushed to see the new-born King. Then the wisemen came, following the star and bearing their gifts to the child, going home a different way for the protection of the baby.

Marty thought that she had never heard anything so beautiful. She couldn't remember ever hearing the complete story before as it was given in the Scriptures. A little baby born in a stable was God's Son. She placed a hand over her own little one.

"Wouldn't be a carin' fer my son to be born in a barn. Don't suppose thet God was a wantin' it thet way either, but no one had room fer a wee baby. Still—God did watch over Him, sendin' angels to tell the shepherds an' all. An' the wisemen too, with their rich gifts. Yes, God was a carin' 'bout his Son."

The story held much appeal for the young woman expecting her first child and she thought on it as she did the dishes. After she was through in the kitchen she returned to the sitting room. Clark had gone out to do up the chores before it got too dark. It was hard enough to see one's way in the daylight in such a storm.

Marty sat down and picked up the Bible. She wished that she knew where to locate the Christmas story so that she might read it again, but as she turned the pages she couldn't find where Clark had read. She did find the Psalms though and read one after the other as she sat beside the warm fire. Somehow they were always so comforting, even when you didn't understand all of the words, she thought.

She read until she heard Clark entering the shed and then laid the Book aside. She'd best put on the coffee and get those 'pickin's' ready.

Later that evening, after Missie had been put to bed, Marty asked Clark shyly if he'd mind reading 'the story' again. As he read she sat trying to absorb it all. She knew a bit more about it this time so could follow with more anticipation, catching things that she had missed the first time. She wondered if Clem had ever heard all of this. It was such a beautiful story.

"Oh, Clem!" her heart cried. "I wisht I coulda shared sech a Christmas with you."

After the reading, Marty sat in silence, only her knitting needles clicking as she worked, for she did not enjoy an evening of idleness, even on Christmas.

Clark crossed to the lean-to and came back with a small package.

"It aint much," he said, "to be a sayin' thank ya fer a carin' fer Missie an' all."

Marty took it from him with a slight feeling of embarrassment. Fumbling, she took off the wrapping to expose a beautiful dresser set, with comb, brush and hand mirror. Handpainted flowers graced the backs in pale golds and oranges. The set itself was ivory in color. It nearly took Marty's breath away.

She turned the mirror over in her hand and noticed initialed on the handle, M.L.C.D. It took a minute for her to realize that they were her initials: Martha Lucinda Claridge Davis. He had not only given her the set, he had given her back her name. Tears pushed out from under her lids and slid unchecked down her cheeks.

"It's beautiful," she whispered, "really beautiful an' I—I jest don't know how to thank ya."

Clark seemed to understand what had prompted the tears.

They had not come until she had read the engraving. He said nothing. Words weren't quite right at such a time.

Marty moved to put the lovely set on her chest in her room. She remembered the scarf. She lifted it out of the drawer and looked at it. No, she decided. She just couldn't. It wouldn't do. She shoved it back in the drawer. It just wasn't good enough, she decided. Not good enough at all.

Chapter 20

A Visit from Ma Graham

Thinking back, Marty declared it a good Christmas in spite of her keen disappointment. It would have been so much fun to have shared it with the Grahams, but there was nothing that could be done about that; and somehow she felt sure that Clark's prayer had been answered and that in years to come they would remember it with warm feelings.

After the storm, the sun came out and the wind stopped howling. The stock moved about again, and the chickens ventured from their coop to their wire enclosure for a bit of exercising. Ole Bob ran round in circles, glad to stretch his legs. Marty envied him as she watched. How good it would be to feel light and easy-movin'.

Looking carefully at herself for the first time in months she studied her arms and hands. They were thinner than they used to be, she realized. She hiked up her skirt and looked at her legs. Yes, she definitely had lost weight, except for the one spot where she had decidedly put it on. She'd have to eat up a bit, she chided herself. She was quite thin enough before. After the baby arrived she'd blow away in the wind iffen she wasn't tied down, as her pa used to say. Well, she was sure enough tied down now, she reasoned. The baby seemed to be getting heavier every day. She felt bulky and clumsy, a feeling that she wasn't used to. Well, she realized, it was to be expected. December was as good as spent. Even as she thought of that with relief, the month of January stretched out before her, looking oh, so long. She wondered if she could endure it. Well, she'd just have to take it one day at a time.

January dawned with a bright sky and no wind, something that Marty had learned to be thankful for. She hated the wind, she decided. It sent chills right through her.

This was the new year. What did it hold for her? A new baby, she hoped. A faint anxiety pressed upon her and she implored Clark's God to please, please let everything be all right.

Clark had been to town again the day before and returned home with a rather grim look. Marty was about to ask the meaning of all of the trips but checked her tongue.

"Iffen it be somethin' I be a needin' to know, he'd be a sayin' so.

"Seems on a new day, of a new year, somethin' good should be happenin'," Marty decided as she went to get breakfast on.

When she checked out the kitchen window she felt that it truly had, for there were three graceful and timid deer crossing the pasture. Marty ran back to the bedroom for Missie.

"Missie," she roused the little girl, "come see."

She hurried back to the kitchen, hoping that the deer hadn't already disappeared. They had stopped and were grazing in an area where horses had pawed the snow from the grass.

"Look, Missie," Marty said pointing.

"Oh-h," Missie's voice held excitement. "Doggies."

"No, Missie," Marty giggled, "it's not doggies. It be deer."

"Deer?"

"That's right. Ain't they pretty, Missie?"

"Pretty."

As they watched, Clark came in from the barn, Ole Bob bounding ahead of him, barking at whatever took his fancy. At the sight of him the deer became instantly alert, long necks stretched up, legs tensed and then, as though on a given signal, they all three leaped forward in long graceful strides, lightly up and over the pasture fence and back into their native woods. It was a breathtaking sight and Marty and Missie

124

were still at the window gazing after them when Clark entered.

"Pa!" cried Missie pointing, "deer—they jump."

"So ya saw 'em, eh?"

"Weren't they somethin'?" Marty said in awe.

"They be right nice all right, though they be a nuisance, too. Been noticing their tracks gettin' in closer an' closer. Wouldn't wonder that one mornin' I be a findin' 'em in the barn with the milk cows."

Marty smiled at his exaggeration. She finally pulled herself away from the window and busied herself with breakfast.

Later in the day, after the dinner dishes had been cleared away and Marty was sitting putting some small stitches on a nightie for the new baby, she heard Ole Bob suddenly take up barking. Someone was coming, she decided, and him not a stranger. She crossed to the window and looked down the road.

"Well, my word," she exclaimed, "it be Ma an' Ben."

Joy filled her as she put aside her sewing and ran to make them welcome.

Clark came in from the yard not seeming too surprised at seeing them.

The men cared for the horses who had worked hard to buck some large drifts across the road. They then seated themselves in the sitting room by the fire and talked of next spring's planting and of their plans to extend their fields, and other man-talk.

"Imagine thinkin' of plantin' now with ten-foot drifts standin' on the corn fields," Marty thought.

The ladies settled in the kitchen. Ma had brought along some knitting and Marty brought out the sock that she was knitting for Clark. She needed help in shaping the heel and was glad for Ma's guidance.

They discussed their Christmases and their disappointment, but both admitted to having a good Christmas in spite of it all. Ma remarked that they were more than happy to say 'yes' when Clark had stopped by yesterday, inviting them to come for coffee New Year's Day if the weather held.

"So thet's it," Marty thought. "An' he didn't tell me fer fear it might be ruined agin by 'mean' weather, as he calls it." The visit took on even more meaning for her.

Ma shared with Marty the news that young Jason Stern was there 'most everytime I turn me round.' With misty eyes she told how Jason had come Christmas Eve and asked permission for Sally Anne and him to be 'a marryin' when the preacher came for his spring visit.

"He seems a right good young man an' I should feel proud-like, but somehow it be hard to give up my Sally, her not yet bein' eighteen, though she will be, jest by the marryin' time."

Marty thought back to her own tearful pleas, begging her ma and pa for permission to marry the young Clem. She was about the age of Sally Anne too. She suddenly saw her own ma and pa in a different light. No wonder they were hesitant. They knew that life could be hard. Still, she was glad that she had had those few happy, even though difficult, months with Clem.

"Thet Jason," Ma went on, "he already be a cuttin' logs fer to build a cabin. Wants 'em ready fer spring so there can be a cabin raisin' an' a barn raisin' too. Workin' right hard he is, an' his pa's a helpin' him. He's gonna farm the land right next to his pa. Well, we couldn't say no, Ben an' me, but we sure gonna miss her happy ways an' helpin' hands. I think it be troublin' Laura, too. She jest not been herself the last few days. Moody an' far-off like. She always was a quiet one, but now she seems all locked up in herself like. Bothers me, it does."

Ma stopped and seemed to look at something a long way off. Then she pulled her attention back to the present.

"We's all gotta settle in an' add to Sally Anne's marriage things—quilts an' rugs an' sech. Got a heap to do twixt now an' spring."

Then Ma changed the subject, catching Marty completely off guard.

"How be things a comin' with the Doc?"

"What Doc?" puzzled Marty.

"Why the one Clark be a workin' on to git to come to town.

The one he be a makin' all the trips fer an' gettin' all the
neighbors to sign up fer. He's most anxious like to git him here
afore thet young'un of yourn makes his appearance."

At Marty's dumb-founded look, Ma finished lamely,
"Hasn't he been a tellin' ya?"

Marty shook her head.

"Hope I haven't spilled the beans," Ma said, "but ever'one
else in the whole west knows 'bout it, seems to me. Thought
you'd be a knowin' too. But then maybe he thought it best ya
not be gettin' yer hopes up. Might be ya jest not mention my
big mouth to him, huh?"

Marty shook her head, dumbly agreeing.

So that was it. All the urgent trips to town and sometimes
beyond, even in poor weather, coming home cold and tired, to
get a doctor to the area before her baby was due. She still
shook her head as she got up to put on the coffee pot. She had
to move quickly before Ma saw her tears.

Lunch was a sumptuous affair. Marty thought back to the
time of Ma's first visit when all that she could offer her was
coffee. How different this was with the abundance of fresh
bread and jelly, fancy cakes, tarts and cookies. Ben remarked
several times about her good cooking and she responded that
she should be, his cook had taught her. Missie wakened and
joined them in her chair, asking for a gingerbread boy. Time
passed all too quickly as they shared table and conversation.

Marty was reluctant to see them go but thankful for the
unexpected time together, and she did want them to arrive
home before night fell.

After they had left she turned happily to cleaning up. Her
eyes twinkled as she turned to Clark.

"Thank ya so much fer invitin' them."

At his surprised look she went on.

"Ma let it slip, not knowin' thet I didn't know." She
couldn't resist adding, "I noticed though thet ya didn't invite
all of those young'uns with the hearty appetites."

They shared a laugh together.

January went crawling by. Clark made more trips to town,
or wherever he went. Marty was no longer puzzled, but she felt

quite sure that he was going off on these cold days on her be-half. Her sewing was nearly completed now and she looked at the small garments, prepared for her coming baby, with much satisfaction. She would be so happy to be able to use the baby things.

Clark fretted about a cradle and Marty assured him that one wasn't needed yet as she planned to take the wee one into her bed until he grew a bit. Clark was satisfied with that, saying that come better weather he'd get busy on a bigger bed for Missie and let the baby take over her crib.

As the month finally drew to a close, Marty felt that the time had come when she could share her secret with Missie. The two of them were alone in the house, Clark having again left for town.

"Come with Mama, Missie," Marty said. "Mama wants to show ya somethin'."

Missie didn't have to be coaxed. She loved to be 'showed somethin'.' Together they went to the bedroom where Marty lifted each tiny garment from the drawer and showed it to Missie. Her face glowed as she did so.

"Look, Missie," she said. "These are fer the new baby. Mama's gonna get a new baby fer Mama and Missie. Jest a tiny little baby, only 'bout so big. Missie can help Mama take care of the baby."

Missie intently watched Marty's face. She wasn't sure what this was all about, but Mama was happy and if Mama was happy, it must be good.

"Ba-by," Missie repeated, stroking the soft things. "Ba-by, fer Mama—an' Missie?"

"Thet's right." Marty was wildly happy. "A baby fer Missie. Look, Missie," she said, sitting on her bed, "right now the baby is sleepin' here."

She laid Missie's hand on her stomach and Missie was rewarded with a firm kick. Her eyes rose to Marty's in surprise as she quickly pulled away her hand.

"Thet's the baby, Missie. Soon the baby will sleep in Mama's bed. He'll come to live with Mama and Missie an' we'll dress 'im in these pretty clothes an' bundle 'im in these soft blankets, an' we can hold him in our arms, 'stead of how Mama be holdin' 'im now."

Missie couldn't get it all, that was for sure, but she could understand that Baby was coming and Mama was glad, and Baby would use the soft things and live in Mama's bed. Her eyes took on a sparkle. She touched Marty timidly and repeated, "Mama's ba-by."

Marty pulled the little girl to her and laughed with glee. "Oh, Missie," she said, "it's gonna be so much fun."

Clark returned home that night with a strange looking lump under a canvas in the back of the sleigh.

"Well," Marty thought, "I'm sure thet be no doctor," and her curiosity was sorely roused.

After Dan and Charlie had been fed and bedded, Clark came through the door carrying the surprise purchase.

A new rocking chair! Marty could scarcely believe her eyes.

"A new rocking chair," she said aloud.

"Right," said Clark. "I vowed long ago thet iffen there ever be another baby in this house, there gonna be a rockin' chair to quiet it by."

He grinned as he said it, and Marty knew that the words were really a 'cover up for other feelings.

"Well," she answered lightly, "best ya sit ya down an' show Missie how it works afore ya go off a chorin'."

Clark did so, pulling Missie up onto his lap and snuggling her down. They took two rocks and the child popped up again to stare at this wondrous thing. She watched, swaying, as Clark rocked a few more times, then snuggled up contentedly, enjoying the new marvel.

Clark soon left for chores and Missie crawled up on her own to try to make the chair respond right.

"It's gonna be so much fun to have," Marty told herself. "Jest imagine me with my young'un all dressed up fancy like, an' me a sittin' there rockin' 'im. I can jest hardly wait."

The baby seemed impatient too, for it gave a hard kick that made its mother catch her breath and move back a mite from the cupboard at which she was working.

When Clark came in from the chores, Missie scooted down from the chair and ran to take his hand.

"Daddy, come," she urged him.

"Hold on, Missie, 'til yer pa gits his coat off," Clark laughed. "I'll come—I'll come."

Missie stepped back and watched him hang up his coat, then took his hand again.

"Come see."

Both Clark and Marty thought that she was still excited about the chair, and it would have been hard to know who was the more surprised when she stopped in front of Marty.

"Look—ba-by," she cried, pointing at the spot. "Ba-by fer Missie."

Marty flushed and Clark grinned.

"Well, I reckon it be at thet," he said, picking up the little girl.

"So Missie is gonna git a new baby, an' we'll rock 'im in the chair," he continued, walking away with the child as he spoke. "We'd better be a gittin' some practice, don't ya s'pose. Let's rock a mite while yer mama gits on the supper."

And they did.

Chapter 21

A New Baby

It was mid-February and Marty sat opposite Clark at the table. Both of them seemed absorbed in their own thoughts. Clark's shoulders drooped slightly. He had failed in spite of all of his efforts. A doctor had been secured for the town and surrounding community, but he wouldn't be arriving until sometime in April—too late for what Clark had wanted him for. He prayed that all would go well.

Marty sat quietly, too, her own thoughts depressed. The little one was getting so heavy, and the last few days things just seemed different. She couldn't name the difference but she knew that it was there. She was troubled in her thinking. This was the time when a woman needed a "real" husband, one that she could talk to. Oh, if only Clem were there. She wouldn't have felt embarrassed to talk it over with Clem.

"I've been a thinkin'," Clark cut in; "seems yer time must be gittin' purty close. Seems ya might feel more easy like iffen Ma could come a few days early an' be a stayin' with ya fer a spell."

Marty hardly dared to hope. "Do ya really think thet she could?"

"Don't know why not. Sally Anne an' Laura be right able to care fer the rest. Good practice fer Sally Anne. Hear she be a needin' to know how afore long. I'll ride over an' have a chat with Ma. I hope we won't be a keepin' her fer too long."

"Oh, me too—me too," thought Marty.

She was so thankful for Clark's words that she had to struggle to keep back the tears.

And so it was that Ma came that day, bringing with her a heavy feather tick and some quilts with which to make up a bed on the sitting-room floor. She was an old pro' at this and Marty took much comfort in the thought.

Marty didn't keep her waiting long. Two mornings after, on February sixteenth, she awoke from a troubled sleep sometime between three and four o'clock. She tossed and turned, not able to find a comfortable position, feeling generally uneasy within herself.

What was uneasiness gradually changed to contractions— not too close and not too hard, but she recognized them for what they were. Around six o'clock Ma sensed more than heard her stirrings and went to her room to see how she was.

Marty groaned. "I jest feel right miser'ble," she muttered.

Ma gently laid a work-worn hand on Marty's stomach and waited until another contraction seized her. "Good," she said. "They be nice an' firm. It be on the way."

Ma hurried out to the kitchen to make sure that the fire that had been banked the night before was still alive. She put in more wood and filled the kettle. She then filled a large pot and placed it on the stove as well. No harm in plenty of hot water. It probably wouldn't be for hours yet, but Ma believed in being prepared.

Hearing the commotion, Clark emerged, already pale-faced, from the lean-to.

"Now ya stop a frettin'," said Ma looking at him. "I know thet she be a little thing, but she be carryin' the baby well. I checked a minute ago. He dropped down right good an' he seems to be turned right. It only be a matter of time 'til ya be a holdin' 'im in thet rockin' chair."

At a cry from Marty, Ma hurried off and Clark sank, even whiter, into a kitchen chair. "Oh, God," he prayed. "It's up to you an' Ma now. I didn't git the Doc, God. Please help Ma now. She's delivered lotsa babies. Help her now with this 'un." There was no Amen, for Clark didn't end his prayer. He continued it on as he went through the trying day.

Missie was bundled up in late morning and sent out with her pa so that she might not hear the agonizing groans of her mama.

Marty carried on, taking one pain at a time, her face damp from the effort, her lips stifling the screams that wanted to come. Ma stayed close by, giving words of encouragement and administering what little comfort that could be given.

Time ticked by so slowly—for Marty who now marked time by contractions; for Clark who, with Missie's help, tried vainly to work on harnesses out in the barn; for Ma who so much wanted the ordeal safely over.

The sun swung around to the west. Would this never end, wondered Marty? It was agonizing. Ma, from her years of experience, knew that the time was drawing near. Everything was in readiness. At fifteen to four, Marty gave a sharp cry that ended as a baby boy made his appearance into the world.

With a sob Marty lay exhausted, so thankful that her work was done, and that Ma's capable hands were there to do what was necessary for the new baby. A glad smile crossed Marty's face as she heard her son cry.

"He's jest fine," Ma said. "A fine big boy."

In short order she had both baby and mother presentable, and placing the wee bundle on Marty's arm went to bear the good news to Clark.

"He's here," she called, "an' he's a dandy."

Clark came running, carrying Missie with him.

"She's okay?" His anxious eyes quizzed Ma.

"Fit as a fiddle," Ma responded, not admitting to any relief on her own part. "She done a great job an' she's got a fine boy. Iffen ya slow down a mite an' take yerself in hand, I may even let ya git a small peek at 'im."

Clark slowed down.

He took off his coat and unbundled Missie, glad that she could now be in. It was getting colder outside.

"Here, Missie, let's warm abit afore we go to see yer mama." They stood together at the fire and then he lifted her up and followed Ma to the bedroom.

Clark looked down on a worn-out Marty. She was tired and

pale and her damp loose hair showed the signs of her tossing, but she smiled up gallantly. His gaze shifted to the small bundle. He was a bit red yet but he sure was one fine boy. One small clenched fist lay against his cheek.

"He's a real dandy," Clark said at last. "What ya be a callin' 'im?"

"He be Claridge Luke," Marty answered.

"Thet's a fine name. What the Luke be for?"

"My pa."

"He'd be right proud could he see 'im. His pa'd be right proud, too, to have sech a fine son."

Marty nodded. The pain was hurting her throat again.

"Claridge Luke Davis." Clark said it slowly. "Right good soundin' name. Bother ya any iffen I shorten it to Clare sometimes?"

"Not a'tall," said Marty. Indeed she wondered if anything would ever bother her again.

They had both forgotten Missie during the exchange, and the little girl remained silent in her pa's arms watching the strange squirming bundle. She noticed that it had on some of the pretty things, and that it was in Mama's bed. At last she inquired, as though trying to sort it out, "Ba-by?"

Clark's attention was brought back to her. "Yah, Missie, baby. That's the baby thet yer mama done got ya. Little Clare, he be."

"Rock—baby?" Missie asked.

"Oh no, not yet awhile," laughed Clark. "First the baby an' yer mama have to have a nice long rest. We'd best be goin' now an' let them be."

Marty answered only with a slight smile. She was a strange mixture of delirious happiness intermingled with sadness, and oh so very tired.

"I do declare," she thought, "I think thet be the hardest work I ever did in my whole lifetime," and after slowly sipping some of Ma's special tea she drifted off to sleep.

Clark continued his prayer. "Thank ya, Father, thank ya for helping Ma, and fer Marty's safe birthin' an' thet fine new boy." This time he said, "Amen."

Chapter 22

Ma Bares Her Heart

Ma stayed on with Marty for a number of days after the arrival of Claridge Luke.

"I wanna see ya back on yer feet like afore I leave ya be," Ma declared. "Sides there be nothin' a pressin' at home jest now."

Marty was more than pleased to have the older woman's company. She was thrilled with her new son and eager to be up and around. Not being one to be happy when kept down, she was at Ma to let her get up from the second day on. Ma, reluctantly at first, allowed her small privileges that gradually grew until she was about again.

Missie was excited about the new baby and loved to share Marty's lap with him as they rocked in the chair. Even Clark seemed to take on a new glow, declaring that "he has already growed half an inch and gained two pounds. I can see it by jest lookin'."

The day soon came when Marty felt sufficiently able to cope with everything on her own. She felt that in spite of Ma's kindness she must be anxious to get home and "look to her own."

Ma nodded her agreement. "Yeah, things do be a goin' fine. Ya take care o' yerself an' things be jest okay. I'll have Clark drive me on home tomorrow."

Marty thought of the morrow with mixed feelings. She

would miss Ma when she left, but it would be good to have her little place all to herself again, too.

That afternoon as they had their coffee together, their conversation touched on many things. They talked of their families and their hopes for the future. Ma again expressed her need to adjust to the fact that her Sally Anne was soon going off on her own.

"She seems so young yet," said Ma. "But ya know ya can't say no once a young 'un has the notion."

"But she's not jest bein' a strong-willed girl," protested Marty; "she jest be in love. Don'cha remember, Ma, what it was like to be so young an' so in love thet yer heart missed beatin' at the sight o' him an' yer face flushed when ya wasn't a wantin' it to? 'Member the wild feelin' thet love has?"

"Yeah, I reckon," Ma said slowly. "Though 'twas so long ago. When I met Thornton, guess I didn't behave myself much better than Sally Anne be a doin.' "

"What was it like, Ma, when ya lost Thornton?"

"When I lost Thornton?" repeated Ma. "Well, it be a long time ago now. But I 'member it still, though it don't pain me sharp like it used to. Myself—way down deep—it wanted to die, too; but I couldn't let it, me havin' three little ones to look to. I kept fightin' on, yet all the time I only felt part there. The rest of me seemed to be missin' or numb or somethin'."

"I know what ya mean," Marty's heart cried.

To Ma she said, "Then ya met Ben."

"Yeah, then I met Ben. I could see he be a good man an' one ya could count on."

"An' ya fell in love with 'im."

Ma shook her head. "No, Marty, there was no face-flushin' an' fast-heart skipp 'n'."

Marty stared.

"No, it be different with Ben. I needed 'im, an' he needed me. I married 'im not fer love, Marty, but fer my young 'uns—an' his."

Ma stopped talking and sat studying her coffee cup, turning it round and round in her hand. "Fact be, Marty." What she was saying, Marty knew was very difficult for her. "Fact be, at first I felt—well, guilty like. I felt like I be a—a loose woman, a sleepin' with a man I didn't feel love fer."

If Ma hadn't been so serious, Marty would have found that statement funny. It was hard to imagine Ma, a steady, solid plain woman, with a faith in God and a brood of eleven, as a loose woman. But Marty did not laugh. She did not even smile. She knew the deep feeling of the other woman.

"I never knowed," she whispered. "I never woulda' guessed thet ya didn't love Ben."

Ma's head jerked up, her eyes wide.

"Lan' sake, girl!" she exclaimed. "Thet were then. Why I love my Ben now, ya can jest bet I do. Fact is, he's been a right good man to me an' I 'spect I love 'im more'n I love myself."

Now it was Marty's turn to show surprise.

"When—when an' how did it happen?" she inquired. "The head spinnin' an' the heart flutterin' an' all?"

Ma smiled.

"No, there never been thet. See—I learnt me a lesson. There's more than one way thet love comes. Oh, sure, sometimes it comes wild-like, makin' creatures into wallerin' simpletons. I've see'd 'im, I've been there myself; but it doesn't have to be thet way, an' it's no less real an' meanin'ful iffen it comes another way. Ya see, Marty, sometimes love comes sorta stealin' up on ya gradual like, not shoutin' bold words or wavin' bright flags. Ya ain't even aware it's a growin' an' growin' an' gettin' stronger until—I don't know. All the sudden it takes ya by surprise like, an' ya think, 'How long I been a feelin' like this an' why didn't I notice it afore?' "

Marty stirred. It was all so strange to get a look inside of Ma like that. She saw a young girl, widowed like herself, with pain and heartache, doing what she had felt was best for her children. And Ma had felt—guilty. Marty shivered.

"I do declare," she thought, "I couldn't have done it. Thanks be to whatever there be, thet I wasn't put in a position like thet. Me, I jest had to be a mama."

She turned from her thoughts, pushing them from her and rose to get more coffee. She didn't want to even think of it anymore. She turned her thoughts to the now. Now Ma was happy again and she needn't feel guilty anymore. She now loved Ben. Just how or when it happened she couldn't really say, but it had. It just—well, it just worked its way into her heart—slowly, softly.

Marty pushed it all aside feeling more at ease with her thoughts at this point, and changed the subject.

The days passed by quickly now. Little Clare was growing steadily and Missie took great pride in her new baby "brudder." Clark was happy to take the young "fella" and rock him if he needed quieting when Marty was busy getting on a meal or doing the dishes. Marty was often tired by the end of the day, but she slept well, even though her sleep was interrupted by night-time feedings.

Clark worked doubly hard on the log cutting. He had confided in Marty that their cabin was too small, and, coming spring, he planned to tear off the lean-to and add a couple of bedrooms. Marty secretly wondered if he had forgotten his promise of the fare for the trip back home. Well, there was plenty of time to remind him of that. It was just the first of March.

Chapter 23

Visitors

A new baby gave the neighbor ladies a valid excuse to put aside the daily duties and go calling, and so it was in the weeks following the arrival of little Clare that Marty welcomed into her home some of her neighbors whom she had not previously known, except perhaps as a face at Clem's funeral.

The first to come was Wanda Marshall. She was small and young, with blond hair that at one time must have been very pretty. She had light blue eyes that somehow looked sad even as she smiled. Marty recognized her as the young woman who had spoken to her the day of Clem's funeral, inviting her to share their one-room home.

Marty set aside the butter she was churning when Mrs. Marshall arrived and welcomed her sincerely. "So glad thet ya dropped by."

Wanda smiled shyly and presented a gift for the new baby.

When Marty opened it, and found a small bib, carefully stitched and with embroidery so intricate she could scarcely understand how one could do such fine work. It looked so delicate and dainty that Marty felt that it resembled the giver. She thanked Wanda and exclaimed over the stitching, to which Wanda gave a slight shrug of her thin shoulders.

"I have nothing else to do."

"Lan' sake," said Marty, "seems I never find time fer

nuthin' since young Clare came along. Even my evenin's don't give me much time fer jest relaxin'.''

Wanda let the comment pass as her eyes searched around the house. She spoke in almost a whisper. "Could I see the baby?"

"My, yes," Marty answered heartily. "He be havin' a sleep right now—he an' Missie—but iffen we tippy-toe in, we can have us a peek. Maybe we'll be able to have us coffee afore he wakes up a wantin' his dinner."

Marty led the way into the bedroom. Wanda looked over at the sleeping Missie with her mussed up curls and sleep-flushed cheeks. "She's a pretty child, isn't she?"

"Missie? Yeah, she be a dollie thet 'un." Marty said with feeling.

They then turned to Marty's bed upon which little Clare was sleeping. He was bundled in the pretty finery that his proud mama had sewn him. His dark head showed above the blanket and, stepping closer, one got a look at the soft pink baby face, with lashes as fine as dandelion silk on his cheeks. The small hands were free and one tiny fist held a corner of his blanket.

Marty thought that he looked beautiful, and wondered that her visitor made no comment. When she looked up it was to see Mrs. Marshall quickly leaving the bedroom.

Marty was mystified. Well, some folks you never could figure. She placed a tender kiss on Clare's soft head and followed her guest back to the kitchen.

When Marty reached the kitchen Mrs. Marshall stood with her back to her, looking out of the window. Marty made no comment but went to add more wood to the fire and put on the coffee. Finally Mrs. Marshall turned slowly to her and Marty saw with surprise that she had been struggling with tears. "I'm sorry," she said with a weak attempt at a smile. "He's—he's a beautiful baby, just perfect."

She sat down at Marty's table, her hands twisting nervously in her lap, her eyes kept low, studying the movement of her hands. When she looked up again, Marty thought that she looked old. With another effort at a smile she went on.

"I'm sorry. I really am. I didn't know that it would be so hard. I mean, I had no idea that I'd react so foolishly. I'd—I'd love to have a baby. My own, you know. Well, I did. I mean—that is, I have had babies of my own—three in fact, but they've not lived—not any of them, two boys and one girl, and all of them—" her voice trailed off; then anger filled her eyes. "It's this wretched country!" she stormed. "If I'd stayed back East where I belong, things would have been different. I would have my family—my Jodi and Esther and Kyle. It's this horrible place. Look—look what it did to you, too. Losing your husband and having to marry a—a stranger in order to survive. It's hateful that's what—just hateful!"

By now the young woman was sobbing, in broken, heart-rending sobs. Marty stood rooted to the spot where she had been standing cutting slices of loaf cake. "Lan' sakes," she said to herself, "the poor thing. What do I do?"

She finally got herself under control and crossed to Wanda, laying a sympathetic hand on her shoulder. "I'm so sorry," she said. "So sorry. Why iffen I'd lost young Clare, I don' know, I jest don' know iffen I could of stood it."

She made no reference to her loss of Clem. This woman was battling with a sorrow that Marty had not had to wage war against—bitterness. Marty continued. "I jest can't know how ya must feel, a loosin' three babies an' all, but I know ya must hurt awful."

By now Marty had placed her arms around the shaking shoulders and pulled the young woman against her. "It's hard, it's truly hard to be a losin' somethin' thet ya want so much, but this I know too: ya mustn't be a blamin' the West fer it all. It could happen anywhere—anywhere. Womenfolk back East sometimes loose their young'uns too. Ya mustn't hate this land. It's a beautiful land. An' you. Yer young an' pretty too, an' ya mustn't let it bitter ya so. Don't do a lick a good to be a fightin' the way things be, when there be nuthin' a body can do to change 'em."

By now Wanda had ceased her sobbing and was allowing herself the comfort of the other woman's words and arms.

"Life be what ya make it, to be sure. No woman could find

good in buryin' three of her babies, but you is young yet, maybe—" she was about to say maybe Clark's God— "maybe the time thet lays ahead will still give ya babies to hold an' love. Ya jest hold on an' keep a havin' faith an' . . . "

Marty's voice trailed off. Land sakes, she didn't know that she could talk on so without stopping.

"An' sides," Marty went on as another thought overtook her, "we're gonna have a doc in town now, an' maybe with his help . . ."

She let the thought lie.

Wanda seemed quieted now. She lay against Marty for a few more minutes; then she slowly straightened. "I'm sorry," she said. "I'm very foolish, I know. You're so kind and so brave, and you're right too—I'll, I'll be fine. I'm glad—about the doctor."

The coffee threatened to boil over and Marty ran to rescue it. As they sat with their coffee and cake they exchanged backgrounds for something to talk about.

Marty learned that Wanda had been a "city girl," well-bred, well-educated, and perhaps a bit spoiled as well. How she ever had gotten way out west still seemed to puzzle her. She shook her head as though she still couldn't quite fathom how it had all come about.

Clare fussed and Marty went to bring him out, nursing him as they continued their visit over their coffee. Not knowing just what effect the baby's presence might have on Wanda, Marty kept him well hidden with the blanket.

Wanda continued on about having so little to do. She did beautiful stitchery, that Marty knew, but she didn't have anyone to sew for. She didn't quilt, she couldn't knit or crochet, and she just hated to cook, so didn't do any more of that than she had to. She loved to read but had read her few books so many times that she practically could recite them and she had no way of getting more.

Marty offered the practical suggestion that she would teach her to quilt, knit or crochet if she cared to learn.

"Oh, would you?" Wanda enthused. "I'd so much love to learn."

"Be glad to," Marty responded cheerily. "Anytime ya care to drop in ya jest come right ahead."

Young Clare finished nursing and set himself to squirming. Marty turned her attention to the baby, properly arranging her clothing and lifting him up for a noisy burp.

Wanda giggled, then spoke softly. "Would you mind if I held him for a minute?"

"Not a 'tall," Marty responded. "Why don't ya jest sit ya there in the rockin' chair a minute. He's already spoiled by rockin', I'm a thinkin', so a little more won't make no difference."

Gingerly Wanda carried the baby to the rocking chair and settled herself with him snuggled up against her. Marty went to clear the table.

When Missie called a few minutes later and Marty crossed through the sitting room to get the little girl, she noticed Wanda gently rocking, eyes far away, yet tender, the young Clare fully enjoying the extra attention.

"Poor thing," Marty's heart responded. "Poor thing. I be jest so lucky."

Ma Graham came next, bringing with her a beautiful handknit baby shawl. Marty declared that she'd never seen one so pretty. Ma brought the youngsters with her on this trip. They all were eager for their first look at their new little neighbor. Ma watched with thoughtful eyes as Sally Anne, eyes shining, held the wee baby close. Each one of Ma's children took a turn carefully holding the baby—even the boys, for they had been raised to view babies as treasures, indeed.

They lunched together and before it seemed possible, the afternoon was gone.

The next day an ill-clad stranger, with two equally ill-clad little girls, appeared at Marty's door. At Marty's welcoming "Won't ya come in," she made no answer, but pushed a roughly wrapped little bundle at Marty.

Marty thanked her and unwrapped the gift to find another bib. It was quite unlike the one that Wanda Marshall had brought—in fact, as different as it could be. The material was coarse, perhaps worn overalling, though the stitches were neat and regular. There had been no attempt to fancy it up, and it looked wrinkled from handling. Marty, however, thanked the woman with simple sincerity and invited them again to come in.

They came in shyly, all three with downcast eyes and shuffling feet.

"I don't remember meetin' ya afore," Marty ventured.

"I be—," the woman mumbled, still not looking up. Marty didn't catch if it was Reno or Tina or what it was, but she did make out Larson.

"Oh, ya be Missus Larson."

The woman nodded, still staring at the floor.

"An' yer two girls?"

The two referred to flushed a deep red, looking as though they wished that they could bury themselves in their mother's wrinkled skirt.

"This be Nandry an' this be Clae."

Marty wasn't sure that she had heard it right, but decided not to ask again.

As they waited for the coffee to boil, Marty took a deep breath and ventured forth. "Be nice weather fer first of March."

The woman nodded.

"Yer man be a cuttin' wood?"

She shook her head in the negative.

"He be a bit down," she finally responded, twisting her hands in her lap.

"Oh," Marty grasped at this. "I'm right sorry to be a hearin' thet. What's he ailin' from?"

Mrs. Larson hunched her shoulders to indicate that it was a mystery to her.

"So be it fer thet," thought Marty.

"Would ya like to see the baby?" she inquired.

The trio nodded.

Marty rose. "He be nappin' now. Come along."

She knew that there was no need to caution for silence.

This ghostly trio was incapable of anything louder than breathing, she was sure.

They reached the bed where young Clare slept and each one of the three raised her eyes from her worn shoes just long enough for a quick look at the baby. Was that a glimmer of interest in the youngest girl's eyes? No, she must have imagined it, Marty decided, and she led the way back to the kitchen.

Marty was never more thankful to see a coffee pot boil in all of her life. Her visitors shyly helped themselves to a cookie when they were passed and seemed to dally over eating them as though to prolong the enjoyment. Marty got the feeling that they didn't have cookies often.

They left as silently as they had come, watching the floor as they said their mumbled good-bye.

Marty crossed to the kitchen window and watched them go.

They were walking. The drifts made the road difficult even for horses, yet they had walked over with their small gift for her baby. The air was cold with a wind blowing and she had noticed that none of her visitors were dressed very warmly. She watched as they trudged through the snow, leaning into the wind, clasping their wanting garments about them, and tears formed in her eyes. She reached for the gift that they had brought with them and suddenly it became something to treasure.

Hildi Stern and Mrs. Watley came together. Hildi was a good-natured middle-aged lady. Not as wise as Ma Graham, Marty told herself, but a woman who would make a right fine neighbor.

Mrs. Watley, Marty didn't hear her given name, was a rather stout, boisterous lady. She didn't appear to be overly inclined to move about too much, and when Marty asked if they'd like to go to the bedroom for a peek at the baby, Mrs. Watley was quick with a suggestion. "Why don't ya jest bring 'im on out here, dear?"

They decided to wait until young Clare finished his nap.

Each lady brought a parcel. Hildi Stern's gift was a small

handknit sweater. Marty was thrilled with it.

Mrs. Watley presented her with another bib. This one was well-sewn and as simple and unfussy as it could be. Marty thanked them both with equal sincerity.

When they had finished their coffee, Mrs. Watley seeming to enjoy her several helpings of cookies and loaf cake, exclaimed rather loudly what a grand little cook Marty was. Next they inspected the new baby. After they pronounced him a fine specimen, saying all of the things that a new mother expected to hear, Mrs. Watley turned to Hildi Stern.

"Why don't ya run along an' git the team, dear, an' I'll be a meetin' ya at the door?'

It was done.

Mrs. Vickers was the last of the neighbor ladies who lived close enough that a new baby merited a drive on the winter roads. She had her boy, Shem, drive her over, and sent him on to the barn with the horses while she came bustling up the walk, talking even before Marty got to the door to open it.

"My, my, some winter we be a havin'. Though I do declare, I see'd me worse—but I see'd me better too—ya can jest count on thet—heerd ya had a new young'un—must be from the first mister, I says, when I hears it—ain't been married to the other one long enough fer thet yet. How it be doin'? Hear he was a healthy 'un—an' thet's what counts, I al'ays say. Give me a healthy 'un any day over a purdy 'un—I al'ays say—take the healthy 'un ever'time—."

She kicked the snow from her boots and went on into the kitchen. "My, my, ain't ya jest the lucky 'un—nice little place here. Sure beats thet covered wagon ya was a livin' in. Not many women here about have a home nice as this, an' ya jest gettin' it all a handed to ya like. Well, let's see thet young-'un."

Marty tactfully suggested that they have coffee while Clare finished his nap, and Mrs. Vickers didn't turn the offer down. She settled herself on a kitchen chair and let her tongue slide over her lips as though adding oil to the machinery so that it would run smoothly.

Marty had opportunity for little more than a slight nod of her head now and then. She thought that maybe it was just as well. If she'd been given a chance for speech, she may have said some unwise things to her visitor.

Between helpings of loaf cake and gulps of coffee, Marty heard that:

"Jedd Larson be nothin' but one lazy good-fer nothin', al'ays gettin' started when ever'one else be done—ceptin' when it come to eatin' or raisin' young'uns—they been married fer ten years—already had 'em eight young'uns—only three thet lived though—buried five—his Missus—so ashamed an' mousy-like—wouldn't no one round even bother to go near—."

Marty made herself a promise that come nice weather she'd pay a call on Missus Larson.

"Thet Graham clan—did ya ever see so many kids in the self-same family? Almost an insult to humans, thet's what it be—bad as cats or mice—havin' a whole litter like thet—."

Marty found herself hard put to hold her tongue.

"See'd thet young Miz Marshall yet? I declare me—thet young prissie would a been better off to stay her back East where she be a belongin'—her an' her first-class airs—an' not even able to raise her a young 'un—woman got no business a bein' out west if they can't raise a young 'un—an' confident like—I think there be somethin' funny there—hard to put yer finger on—but there all the same—doesn't even give ya a proper welcome when ya call—me, I called, neighbor-like when each of the young 'uns died—told her right out what she prob'ly be a doin' wrong—well, ya know what—she most turned her back on me—."

Poor Wanda, thought Marty, aching for her.

"Well, now—if that's the way she be, I says, leave her to it. Have Hildi and Maude been over? I see'd 'em go by t'other day—goin' over to see thet new young 'un of the Davis', I says to myself—well, Hildi be a fine neighbor—though she do have some strange quirks—me, I'm not one to be a mentioning 'em. Maude Watley now—thet be another matter—wouldn't do nothin' thet took any effort, thet one—she wasn't always big

as the West itself—be there a time afore she catched her man
thet she be a dance-hall girl—she wouldn't want one a knowin'
it o' course—but it be so—have ya been to town yet?"

At Marty's shake of her head, she hurried on.

"Well, mind ya, when ya do go, don't ya be a tellin' nuthin'
to thet there Miz McDonald thet ya don't want spread round
thin like. She be a first rate tongue-wagger, thet 'un."

Marty also heard that:

Miz Standen, over to town, had her a Saturday beau.

She be a bettin' thet the visitin' parson had him somethin'
to hide, or he'd settle himself to one place.

The Krafts were expectin' them another young 'un—
makin' five.

Milt Conners, the bachelor of the area, seemed to be gettin' stranger ever'day. Should git 'im a woman—thet would be
doin' him some good—he was gettin' likker somewhere too—
nobody knowed where but she had her s'pisions.

The new doc be arrivin' in April—folks a sayin' thet Clark
bought 'im—well—they needed a doc—jest hoped he was
worth it an' not here jest to make money on people's woes.

Young Sally Anne was hitchin' up with Jason Stern—supposed those two families be a pairin' off regular like in the next
few years.

She finally stopped for a breath, and Marty wondered
aloud that Shem had not come in from the barn, and supposed
that he was getting cold and tired of waiting. Well, she'd send
a slice of cake and a gingerbread cookie or two out with Mrs.
Vickers.

Mrs. Vickers took the hint and took her leave, still chattering as she left, leaving Marty's head spinning and her ears tin-
gling. She hadn't even looked at the baby.

Chapter 24

New Discoveries

The days of March were busy days for Clark. He pushed himself hard at the logging, working as long as there was light and doing the chores with the aid of the lantern. Each night at the supper table he tallied up his total for Marty to share and together they kept track of how many more logs were needed.

Marty's days were full too, doing the usual housework and caring for the new baby and Missie. It was hard for her to get the clothes dry from one washing to the next.

In the evenings both Clark and Marty were happy to rest a spell before the open fire, Marty with her quilt pieces or knitting, Clark with one of his books, or light work of one kind or another. Marty found it increasingly easy to talk to Clark. In fact, she looked forward to relating the events of the day.

Clark had spent many evenings fashioning a new bed for Missie so that the fast-growing Clare would be able to take over the crib. Marty enjoyed watching the bed take shape. The few simple tools that Clark worked with responded well to his capable hands. She carefully pieced the quilt that would go on the bed and felt a real sense of a joint accomplishment.

As they worked, they talked, sharing small events that made up their little world. The early fall and long winter had brought the animals down from the hills in search of food. Lately a couple of coyotes had been moving in closer and closer at nights, causing poor Ole Bob a great deal of noisy concern.

The neighbors were rarely seen during the winter months so news was scarce. Measles had been reported in the town, but no serious cases had been heard of.

They talked of the spring planting and the plans for the new breaking, of the hope that spring would be early rather than late in coming. They shared the "cute" things that Missie said and the progress report of Clare. It was the "little things" that they discussed in their evenings, yet in doing so they were discovering deeper things about each other without realizing it. Feelings, dreams, hopes and faith were shared in a relaxed, simple way.

One evening, as Marty quilted and Clark sanded the headboard for the bed, their talk turned to the scripture that they had read at breakfast that morning. A lot of the words were without meaning to Marty, with her having no background in such things. Clark explained very simply the promises to the Jewish people of a Messiah who would come. Their understanding of His purpose in coming was far different from what He actually came to accomplish. They wanted freedom from Rome: He came to give freedom from self. They wanted to be part of a great earthly kingdom, but His kingdom was a heavenly one.

Marty began to understand some of the things concerning Him, but there were still a lot of unanswered questions in her mind.

"Do ya really think thet God, who runs the whole world like, be a knowin' you?" she asked.

"I'm right sure thet He do," Clark responded simply.

"An' how ya be so sure?"

"Cause He answers so many of my prayers."

"Ya mean by a givin' ya whate're ya ask fer?"

Clark thought a minute, then shook his head.

"No, not thet. Ofttimes He jest helps me to git by without what I asked fer."

"Thet be strange talk."

"I'm a thinkin' not. A lot of times, what folks ask fer, they don't a'tall need."

"Like what?"

"Like good crops, new plows, an extry cow or two."

"What about iffen ya lose something thet ya already had an' had sorta set yer mind on?"

"Ya mean like Clem or Ellen?"

Marty nodded slowly.

"He don't take away the hurt, but He shares it with ya."

"Wisht I woulda had me someone to share mine with."

"He was there, an' I'm a thinkin' thet He helped ya more than ya knowed."

"But I didn' really ask Him to."

"I did."

Chapter 25

Fire!

On March sixteenth little Clare marked his first month in the family. So far he had been a first-rate baby, but, as Clark kept warning, "Jest ya wait 'til he starts cuttin' his teeth."

Marty hoped that Clark would be wrong—and so did Clark.

The day had been colder again, and it looked like another storm might be due so Clark had left early in the morning to restock their supplies.

He was back earlier than usual and the feared storm was still holding off. Mrs. McDonald had sent a small parcel for the baby. Marty opened it excitedly and found another small bib.

"I do declare," she laughed. "Thet boy sure be well set up fer bibs. Guess he be well fixed fer droolin'."

Clark laughed with her.

Missie's bed had been completed now and set up in the bedroom, and the small crib was moved into the sitting room where it was warmer for the baby during the day. He was awake more now and liked to lie and look around, waving his small fists frantically in the air. Marty still took him to bed with her at night.

The day ended and evening fell with a shift in the wind. Observing it, Clark said, "Guess we not be gettin' thet storm tonight after all."

The thought was a pleasant one. Large drifts of snow lay over the ground and hopes for an early spring were being shattered daily. The weather stayed cold with occasional snow flurries, and cold winds made winter's long stay even more unwelcome.

They were both tired from a long day's work, Clark having hurried his trip to town and Marty having done her bread baking as well as washing for the baby, so they retired a bit earlier than the usual.

Marty tucked herself in, stretching her toes deep into the warm blankets. She nursed young Clare so that he would sleep as far into the night as possible, and settled down with him on her arm.

She felt that she had barely fallen into a deep sleep when she was awakened. Clark was bending over her, pulling on his jacket as he spoke hurriedly.

"The barn be ablaze. Ya jest stay put. I'm goin' fer the stock," and he was gone.

Marty's head whirled. Had she had a dream? No, she was sure that he had really been there. What should she do? It seemed like eons before she finally moved, though in truth it was a matter of seconds. She jumped from her bed, not stopping to dress herself or even to slip into her house-socks. She ran through the house to the kitchen window. Before she even arrived she could see the angry red glow. Horror struck her as she looked at the scene. There was the barn, roof aflame with angry leaping fire, the smoke pouring forth, darkening the sky, and there was Clark taking the last few steps in long, running strides. He swung open the barn door and smoke gushed out.

As Marty realized what he had said to her and saw him about to carry it out, her own voice choked her. "No, Clark, no. Don't go in there, please, please—."

But he had gone—for the animals. They could get more animals—.

Marty stood silently, only because her words refused to come—watching, straining, dying a thousand deaths in what seemed forever, praying as best she could. And then, through the smoke plunged Charlie—or was it Dan—and right behind him came the other horse, rearing and pawing the air. The saddle horse came close behind, dragging his halter rope, tossing his head wildly, running until he crashed stupidly into the corral fence, falling back only to struggle up again and race on.

Marty stood staring at the door. "Oh, Clark, Clark, please, please. God, iffen yer there, please let 'im come out."

But the next dark figure to come through the smoke was a milk cow, then another, and another.

"Oh, God!" sobbed Marty, "he'll never make it."

The walls of the barn were engulfed in flame now, too. The fire licked hungrily along the wall reaching out toward the door. And then she saw him, stumbling through the entrance, dragging harnesses with him, staggering along until he reached the corral fence where he leaned for support, pulling the wet towel that he had hurriedly grabbed on his way out, from his head and face so that he might breathe more freely.

"Oh, God!" cried Marty, as she collapsed in a heap on the cold kitchen floor.

Somehow the long night blurred on. Marty's senses didn't seem to be taking it all in. Clark was safe, but the barn had gone. Neighbor men, with water and snow, seemed to be everywhere, fighting to save the other buildings.

Women were there, too, busy about her, bustling, talking, giving the men a hand by turns, making up sandwiches and coffee. Marty felt numb. Someone placed baby Clare in her arms.

"He's cryin' to eat," they said. "Best ya sit ya down an' nurse 'im."

She did. That much she could understand.

Morning came. The barn lay in smouldering ruins, but the other buildings had been saved.

The tired, smokey faces gathered in the yard for the coffee and sandwiches. Their clothes and boots were ice-crusted, their hands cupped around the mugs for warmth. They talked in hushed tones, for losing one's barn and feed, with winter still present, was a great loss and each one knew it well.

After having gulped the coffee, they gathered their women, anxious to be home and out of their frozen clothing. Just as the first team left the yard, Jedd Larson turned his team in.

"Good ole Jedd," Marty heard a cross whisper. "Probl'y be late fer his own buryin'."

Jedd took over where the others had left off, helping himself to a cup of coffee, and finishing up the sandwiches. As the neighbors, one by one, took their leave he appeared to be settling in for a long stay.

"Poor Clark," Marty thought as she glanced anxiously out the kitchen window. "He jest be lookin' beat. All ashes an' soot an' half-frozen, an' now Jedd wants to sit an' chaw him to death—no sense a'tall, thet Jedd. Well, I won't 'llow it," and pulling her shawl about her shoulders she marched out.

"Mr. Larson," she greeted the man. "Right good of ya to be comin' over to give us a hand. Guess things be under control like now, thanks to all our fine neighbors. Have ya had coffee? Good! I'm sorry to be interruptin' like, but right now I'm afeared thet my husband be needed indoors—iffen ya be excusin' 'im."

She had never referred to Clark as her husband before and if she had been watching, she would have seen a surprised look on his face, but he said nothing. She motioned toward the door. Clark muttered his thanks to Jedd and went into the house.

"Give yer Missus our greetin's. We won't be a keepin' ya any longer, ya havin' chores to home a waitin' on ya an' all. Ya'll be pleased to come agin when ya can sit an' chat a spell. Thank ya agin. One really 'preciates fine neighbors. I'd best be gettin' in to my young 'uns. Good day, Mr. Larson."

Marty returned to the house. Jedd Larson crawled into his wagon and went home. He didn't have the wagon box moved to the sleigh runners yet. Kept planning on getting to it but just hadn't found the time.

Marty returned to the house to find a puzzled Clark. He had gone all through the house twice looking for who or what he was needed for but had found nothing. Missie, whom he had expected to find in hysteria, lay sleeping soundly, untouched by the night's drama. Clare was not sleeping, but lay contentedly sucking a fist.

As Marty came in Clark looked at her. "Who be needin' me?" he asked, and she noticed that his lips had cracked from the heat.

She stared at him dumbly. She had fought bravely through the night, answering their questions of where to find the coffee and all and was she okay. She had restrained herself from running out to the yard to see if Clark was really all right. She had kept from striking out at whoever or whatever had let such a disastrous thing happen to Clark, he who worked so hard, who helped his neighbors, who talked quietly and never lost his temper, who didn't drink or beat his woman, who believed in God and prayed to Him daily, who lived by the Book and what it said. Why, why did it happen to him? Why not lazy Jedd Larson or—or—. After fighting all night, and winning, Marty could fight no more. She turned from him, leaned against the wall, and let the sobs shake her body.

She felt his hands on her shoulders as he turned her to him, then pulling her gently into his arms, he held her close like a weeping child, stroking her long loose hair. Silently he let her weep until all of the confusion and anger had drained from her. Finally she was able to stop. She pulled herself away, wiping her face on her apron. "Oh, Clark," she whispered, "what aire we gonna do now?"

He didn't answer for a moment and then he spoke so calmly that she knew that he felt sure of his answer. "Well, we aire gonna pray, an' what He sees us to be a needin', He'll give; an' what He see we don' need, He'll make us able to do without."

They bowed their heads together.

Chores that morning were a burdensome affair. The cows in their terror had run off. The horses, too, had scattered. The pigs were safe in their pens, as were the chickens; but Clark was hard put finding enough to satisfy them without digging too deeply into the precious seed grain. The grazing stock, one pasture over, stood in their shelter bawling to be fed, but with what? All of their feed had gone up in smoke. After doing the best that he could, Clark came in for breakfast.

Marty fretted over his cracked lips and blistered hands,

but Clark lightly brushed aside her concern.

After their morning reading and prayer they began their meal. Missie was strangely quiet, sensing that something was amiss. Finally Marty could stand it no longer. "What ya plannin' to do?"

"First off, I'm goin' over to Ben's. He said he'd be right glad to take two of the milk cows. He'll feed 'em both in exchange fer the milk from the one ther's still milkin'. When I have me feed again, we'll get 'em back."

"An' the rest of the stock?"

"We'll have to be a sellin' the fifteen head in the grazin' pen."

"An' the hogs?"

"Most of 'em will have to go. I hope to spare me a young sow or two."

"How ya be a feedin' 'em?"

"The seed grain wasn't lost. It's in the bins by the pig lot. I'll have to hold me off plantin' thet new land I'd been a countin' on 'til another year, an' use some of the grain to feed a sow through."

"An' the horses?"

"Horses aire fair good at grazin' even in the winter. They can paw down through the snow. I'll take me a bit of money from the sellin' of the stock to git me enough feed to look to the one milk cow thet we keep."

"Ya got it all figured already."

"Not quite all, but I been workin' on it. We maybe have to skimp a bit here an' there, but we'll make it. Iffen all goes well, come crop time, we'll be gettin' on our feet agin."

"An' the fare back east?" Marty didn't ask this out loud, but Clark somehow must have seen the question in her eyes.

He looked deeply at her for a moment, then spoke slowly. "When I asked ya to set yerself in here to care fer Missie, I made a promise to ya. I'm not a goin' back on it now. Tell ya the truth, I would be a missin' ya should ya go, you an' the young 'uns, but I'll not be a holdin' ya iffen it's what ya be a wantin'."

For the first time Marty was no longer sure.

Clark carried his plans through for the stock. The hogs, except for two promising young sows, were sold, as was the grazing stock. It was decided to buy enough feed for the milk cow and the two sows, and to save the seed grain so that the new field could be sown. They would need the money from the crop more than ever to help with expenses until the livestock built up again. Only a few hens were saved. The rest were put in crates and taken to town.

Clark now had more logs to cut, as come spring a new barn would have to be built.

The corral fence was repaired and the single cow and team of horses were placed in the grazing pen where there was a shelter for them. The saddle horse was lent to Jason Stern, who seemed to have great need of it for the present.

Somehow life fell into a routine again. No one wished for spring more fervently than Marty.

Chapter 26

Barn Raisin'

March blew itself out in an angry swirl and April came in, promising better things in the days ahead. As the month grew older the snow began to disappear, the sun took on new warmth, and patches of green slowly began to appear in sun-warmed places. Dan and Charlie sought out each patch, eager for easier feeding. The milk cow had ceased milking, readying herself for calving. Milk now had to be brought by pail from the Grahams every few days.

Near the end of the month, Marty looked out at the nearly bare steaming garden. How eager she was to get at the planting. She had been cooped up for so long, and could hardly wait to get out into the warm sunshine, to some task that could be done out of doors.

However, there were other things that must be done before spring planting. Over the month the neighbor men had taken their teams and given Clark a hand with the logging. Now the logs stood ready for the raising of the new barn. If they had a good day, they'd even give a hand with the two bedrooms, they had promised.

Marty looked out now, envisioning the new barn standing where the old one had stood. How good it would be to see Clark have a barn again. The bedrooms—she'd wait for them if she had to.

But the first big event was to be the house raising for young Jason Stern and Sally Anne, a house being even more important to a man than a barn. Tomorrow was set aside for the "raisin'," and Marty had been busy draining kraut, cooking ham, and baking extra bread and pie. The men would share their labors and the womenfolk would share their larders. Marty looked forward to the day. It would be so good to have a visit with her neighbors.

The house raisin' went well and the men finished the task in the late afternoon. The women enjoyed a day visiting and sharing recipes and patterns. The Larsons were late and when they did arrive, Mrs. Larson shyly shoved her pot of potato stew onto the table laden with good things. The womenfolk for the most part didn't seem to notice hef, but Marty crossed over to her to at least say a "howdy."

Jedd was there only to give a hand on the last few logs, but then seemed to consider his advice of far more worth than his brawn. He did, however, manage a hearty meal along with the rest.

Marty went home, contented. Sally Anne would have a nice little cabin to set up housekeeping in. True, there was still a lot that needed to be done, but Marty was sure that in Jason's eagerness he'd soon take care of that.

Marty had had a nice long visit with Wanda Marshall, showing her a simple crochet pattern and finding her a keen pupil.

Mrs. Vickers had buzzed about, whispering choice bits in various ears, and Mrs. Watley had planted herself in a sunny spot by the desserts and busied herself with drinking coffee and "keepin' the young 'uns outen the food."

It was all fun, Marty decided, and next week it would be their turn.

True to their word the neighbors arrived on Tuesday morning with a determination to get the job done. Log by log the barn began to raise. Clark and Todd Stern manned the axes that skillfully cut the grooves so that one log might fit the next.

By the time the women banged on a pot to announce dinner, the barn had taken on shape, nearly reaching the rafter stage. The men were eager to get back to their work so did not tarry long over their meal.

While the women were doing the dishes, Tommy Graham came in. "Pa said, iffen ya be a movin' the things from the lean-to, we be a tearin' it off an' makin' the bedrooms."

Marty fairly flew. She had never been in the lean-to before, and was a bit shocked at its barrenness. The bed frame held a coarse straw tick. Marty thought it hard and lumpy. Thoughts of her own soft feather tick made her feel guilty. The few articles that Clark had were quickly moved into the sitting room, as well as his clothes from the pegs.

Marty was scarcely finished when she heard the hammers and crowbars. The men went to work with a will and by supper time the logs were in place.

Supper was almost festive. The men felt well pleased with themselves. Clark Davis was a favorite neighbor. There wasn't a man there that he hadn't helped out at one time or another, and it pleased them to be able to help him in return.

When the meal was over the men visited while the women cleaned up the tables and sorted out their own crockery and pans.

Jedd had really set a new record on that day. He had made it in time for both dinner and supper, partaking freely of both meals. His Missus couldn't make it, feelin' poorly. Marty felt sorry for the poor woman.

At last they were all gone, some having promised to be back to help with the roofing and the floors.

Clark was half-dead on his feet, wanting to carry more than his share of the load on his own "raisin' " and then having to do up the chores after the others had left. He stretched out on the hard straw tick on the sitting-room floor, meaning to just rest a bit before he went to bed "proper like" and in next to no time was sound asleep.

Marty, who came through from the kitchen, stopped short. "Lan' sakes," she exclaimed, "he be plum' beat."

She crossed to gently ease a pillow under his head and slip off his shoes, then, placing a blanket over him, she went on to bed.

Chapter 27

Laura

In less than two weeks' time the visiting preacher would be paying his visit and Sally Anne would be marrying. Ma hated to think of it, but she guessed that it was a part of life, and from now on she'd be losing them one by one.

The thought of Sally Anne leaving the nest was one that she could accept, but Laura's strange behavior troubled her. The girl had been acting so differently lately, sullen and resentful around the house, then slipping away for long walks. At times she even rode off on one of the work horses.

Finally Ma could take it no longer and knew that she must have a talk with the girl. She waited for a time when they were alone, then began as gently as she could.

"Laura, I be thinkin' thet somethin' be a troublin' ya. I'd be right glad to be a sharin' it iffen ya'd like to lay it on me."

Laura looked at her with rebellion in her eyes.

"Nothin' the matter with me," she responded hotly.

"I think there be. Maybe it be a natural thing—all the fussin' an' fixin' fer Sally Anne."

Laura's chin went up. "What care I 'bout Sally Anne?"

"She be yer sister—"

"No, she ain't."

Ma looked fully at the girl now. Anger began to take her.

"Ya listen here, Missie. Sally an' you been close like ever since I be yer Ma."

"Ya ain't my Ma."

Ma stopped short, her mouth open. She had known that things were bad, but had not guessed that they were this bad. Finally she started over slowly. "Laura, I'm sorry, really I am. I never knowed ya felt this way—so strong like. I've tried to be a ma to ya. I love ya like ya was my own, and yer pa—he'd do most anythin' fer ya."

"Won't need to be a doin' fer me much longer now," declared Laura.

"Whatcha meanin'?"

"I'm a gettin' married too."

"Yer gettin' married? But ya ain't even had ya a beau."

"Have too."

"Well, we never knowed it. Who be—?"

"Milt Conners!"

Ma gasped. Never in her life would she give one of hers to that drinking, no-good, ruffian, Milt Conners. Not if her life depended on it.

When finally she could speak again, she tried her hardest to be firm yet gentle. "Oh, no ya ain't. No one in this house be a takin' themselves up with Milt Conners. Iffen I didn't stop ya, yer pa sure would."

"Ya can't stop me!" Laura exploded.

"Oh, yes'm we can," said Ma, equally determined, her usually gentle eyes gleaming.

"It be too late," flung out Laura.

"Whatcha be a meanin'?"

"I'm—I'm gonna have his baby."

Ma staggered forward a step and steadied herself with her hands on the back of a chair. "Whatcha be a sayin', girl?"

Laura stood her ground. Let Ma fume and fuss, or beat her or anything. Come time for Sally Anne to be a standing before the preacher, she'd be there, too.

"I'm gonna have his baby," she repeated.

Ma stepped forward, her face white. Tears already showed on her cheeks. She reached out for Laura and pulled her gently into her arms, holding her close, her head bowed against the long brown hair.

"Oh, my poor baby," she wept; "my poor, poor baby."

Laura hadn't expected the tears nor the deep love, and for a moment she nearly gave in.

She hated to tell Ma a lie, but she knew that under no other circumstances would Ma or her pa allow her to marry Milt Conners. No, she'd just have to go through with it and let the future take care of itself.

The two weeks until the preacher's visit went very quickly. When Sally Anne heard of Laura's planned wedding, she offered to share some of her own prepared household articles. Laura would have none of them, declaring that she wouldn't need much as Milt was already set up for housekeeping. Nevertheless, Ma sat up until late each night, making quilts and hemming towels and curtains.

Ben carried on his usual work, but his shoulders sagged, and his face appeared drawn. The anticipation of the big day had been robbed from them. Even Laura did not take on the glow that a new bride should, but she set her jaw determinedly, and helped in the preparations for the weddings.

Chapter 28

The Big Day

The preacher's visit was to be made on Easter Sunday morning. They would first have an outdoor service together, then the wedding ceremonies would follow. Later the neighbors would all join together for a potluck dinner to honor the new couples and to have a chance for a neighborly visit before spring work would demand all their time.

Marty looked forward to the day. It would be good to see the neighbors that she had come to know. Winter had seemed to stretch on for such a long time and the feeling of spring in the air made her restless to get out, somewhere—for something. She was curious about the church service and what the preacher would have to say. She had never been in a service just for preachin' before. Her only connection with church had been for marriages and funerals.

She felt happiness for Sally Anne with the sparkle of love on her face, but her heart ached for Laura. Ma had confided with a troubled and heavy heart the reason for the consent to the marriage. Marty shared Ma's concern over the coming union and felt such a helplessness, knowing that there was nothing that any of them could do to prevent possible heartache from reaching out to the strong-willed girl.

Marty busied herself embroidering two sets of pillow cases for the new brides. She was fearful lest her feelings even show themselves in her stitching. The one pair was so much fun to work. The other made even her fingers feel clumsy and heavy.

The days ticked off quickly and the big day arrived. The sun was up and promised a warm spring day as Marty bustled about readying the pots of food that she would be taking and getting Missie and Clare dressed in their finest.

She would wear her yet unworn blue-grey dress. She finally knew that she would feel "right" in it. Clark did look at her with admiration and she flushed under his gaze. At last they were all packed up and on their way.

Marty's eyes shone as she faced the bright morning, noticing each new sign of spring around her. The fields were now bare, with only patches of dirty snow left in hidden places. The first flowers were slowly lifting their heads to the sun. Returning birds occasionally made an appearance on a fence post or tree limb. But the surest sign of spring was the feeling within her as she breathed in deep draughts of the warm, fragrant air. It was so good just to be alive.

They were one of the first families to reach the Grahams, and Marty hurried in to help Ma with the last of the preparations. Clark assured her that Missie and Clare would be fine left with him; the fresh air would do them all good. As Marty turned to hurry into the house, she heard Ben's comments on what a fine looking son Clare was becoming and Clark's light boasts of his already apparent strength and awareness. Marty smiled to herself.

Make-shift benches had been placed for the church service, and long tables had been arranged for the dinner meal.

Ma's house was a hive of activity, for a visit from the preacher and two weddings on the same day were cause for any amount of flurry.

The Sterns arrived, causing Sally Anne to flush a becoming shade. Jason looked at her with pride in his eyes.

Just before the service was to begin, Milt Conners appeared, looking as sullen and troublesome as ever. He was welcomed by the men who made room for him on the bench, but Marty again felt the stirrings of alarm within her. She could not feel at ease about this man.

After all were seated on the benches, Ben Graham stood to his feet and welcomed the neighbors to his farm on this "fine spring day." He trusted that they would find the Easter service a "real blessin' " and welcomed them to share in the weddings of his two eldest daughters, and thanked them kindly "fer all the good food appearin' on the tables."

He then welcomed the visiting preacher, Parson Simmons, and expressed how "fine it is to have 'im here on Easter Sunday mornin', an' I know we's all lookin' forward to sharin' in the mornin' meetin'."

The preacher took over then and commented on the "beautiful day that the Lord hath made," expressed his delight at seeing them all in attendance and led the group in prayer. They then sang a few hymns from memory, not having any hymnals. Marty didn't know the words to any of the hymns, but she enjoyed listening to the others sing. She must get Clark to teach her some of the words to the songs, she decided.

When Parson Simmons began to speak to the people, Marty listened intently. It was the simple story of Easter that he related, beginning with Christ's ministry to the people of His day, His arrest and the false accusations that sentenced Him to die. The preacher told of the surface reasons for His death and then explained the real purpose in the Father allowing, yea, planning for it to be so.

Marty's heart was torn as she listened to the words. She had heard before how cruel men of Christ's day had put Him to death with no just cause, but never before had she realized that it had anything at all to do with her. Now, the fact that He personally took the punishment for her sins, as well as for the sins of all mankind, was a startling and sobering discovery.

"I didn't know—I jest didn't know thet ya died fer me," her heart cried. "I'm sorry—truly I am. Lord, I asks ya to be a doin' what yer intendin' in my heart." Big tears slipped from her eyes and down her cheeks. She didn't even bother to wipe them away. Clark's eyes filled with concern as he glanced her way.

But the preacher did not stop there. He went on with the

story of that first Easter morning when the women went early to the tomb and found that the Lord had risen.

"He lives," said the preacher, "and because He is victor over sin and death, we too can be."

Marty's heart filled with such a surge of joy that she felt like shouting—but not here—not now, she cautioned herself. She would though. She had to tell someone that now she understood. She had given herself to be a knowin' Clark's God.

She reached down and slipped her small hand into his strong one. Clark looked at her, reading the difference in her face, and the big hand firmly clasped the small one. Marty knew that he shared her joy, as she now shared his God. It was enough.

The marriages followed the worship service. Laura and Milt were first. Sally Anne wanted it that way. Milt looked down at his feet, which shifted back and forth with regularity. His clothing looked unkept, though he had trimmed his beard and had a haircut. Laura looked shyly at him in a way that made Marty hope that maybe with the help of a good woman's love, this man could indeed change. She hoped with all her heart that the two could find happiness together.

Jason and Sally Anne were next and Marty felt that the joy and love that showed on their faces was reflected in her own heart. How easy it was to share in their happiness.

As soon as the ceremonies were over, the neighbors began merry-making, throwing rice, ringing cowbells and lining up to kiss the brides. The two couples were finally allowed to sit down at the table piled with gifts, and while the womenfolk made preparations for the noon meal, the brides unwrapped the presents.

The meal was a plentiful one and each person there was feeling especially joyous. Spring was here, they had just heard again the story of Easter, they had witnessed two marriages, they could enjoy a feast with good neighbors—life was full. As the good-natured talk and laughter carried on, the Larsons arrived. Jedd did not bother to tether his team. Mrs. Larson placed a pan of cornbread on the heavy-laden table and then with eyes to the ground ushered her youngsters to a safe-looking far table. Marty rose from her place and with a pretense of refilling the water pitcher, passed by close, hoping to share a smidgen of the new-found concern she felt.

"Ya all be welcome. So glad ta see ya agin." The woman did not lift her eyes, but a small spot of color appeared in each cheek as she answered the greeting. "The good Lord 'as done so much fer all of us," Marty continued, reaching out to tossle each child's hair. "Preacher talk'd 'bout it this mornin', how's God can clean up folks' hearts and change their ways. Jest sets ya ta bubblin'."

Marty's feelings soared with satisfaction as she noticed Mrs. Larson's upward glance. Wasn't that an expression of hope? Meanwhile, Jedd just loaded his plate and settled down to eat. The talk could come later.

When the tables had been cleared away and the two young couples had loaded their wagons and kissed Ma good-bye, Clark and Marty lingered for a while, sensing just how difficult the time was for Ma and Ben.

Ma bore up bravely but there was a longing look in her eyes as she kissed Sally Anne good-bye, and a look of deep concern as she pulled Laura close to her, holding her long before she released her. Marty turned away lest her own tears spill over.

Chapter 29

Planting

The sun seemed to carry more warmth each day. Clark had finished his work on the new bedrooms and was busy tilling the fields. Each day saw more land prepared for the seed that would be sown.

There was enough grass now for the three cows to find fair grazing. A young calf was in the weaning pen, the second cow was still to calf, the third would be much later.

One of the sows had piglets at her side. She had not given them as good a litter as they had hoped for, having only six and losing two, but they hoped that the second sow would do better. Marty had three of her eight hens on settings of eggs. She hoped to replenish the chicken coop again.

The barn stood straight and strong where it had been rebuilt. It was a bit larger than its predecessor. As yet it was still unchinked, but that could be done in a slack time. The roof was on, the floor in, and it would do as it was until after the crop was in the ground.

Marty hummed as she made the breakfast pancakes. It had been several mornings since they had had pancakes, and Missie had asked for them. As Marty stirred her batter she wondered how the two-week old brides were making out with their cooking. She was sure that they would do much better than what she had done. Ma would have prepared them well.

She heard that Sally Anne was well settled-in. She and Jason had driven over one evening to return the saddle horse. Jason's eyes shone with pride as he boasted of how Sally Anne had hung the curtains, spread the rugs and set her little kitchen in order. She was a right fine cook too, he went on, and Sally Anne's cheeks had flushed with pleasure at the boasting. Clark and Marty spoke of it later with amusement. Marty smiled now at the thought of the young couple so content in their love for one another.

Then her thoughts shifted to Laura. How was Laura really doing, she wondered? Clark had seen her on the road once as he came from town. He had driven up over the brow of a sharp hill and there was Laura walking down the road. She had seemed startled at his sudden appearance, he said, and had turned sharply away. When he stopped the team to offer her a lift, she looked back at him to say a "no thanks, walkin' be right good for me." But her eyes looked troubled and there was a bruise on her cheek. He had gone on his way, but as he related his story to Marty that evening she could tell that he was deeply troubled by it all. Poor Laura, Marty thought, shaking her head. To be expecting a child with this man and seeming so unhappy and alone. Her heart ached for her.

She could hear Clark's whistling as he came from the barn, so hurried with the finishing of the breakfast preparations. "I wonder," she thought, "if spring plantin' always makes a man so happy like."

Spring was getting into her blood, too, and she was anxious to get her own hands into the soil. It was so wonderful to feel light and slim again. She felt that she could fairly glide as she moved about, airy and sure-footed, not weighted down and clumsy with the carryin' of a young 'un. She was once again thankful to have baby Clare out where she could hug him close or lay him down at will, rather than carrying the heavy little burden with her everywhere.

During morning reading and prayer Marty understood in a new way the meaning of Jesus' words, "Come to me, all who labor and are heavy laden, and I will give you rest."

"I thank ye, Lord, that ye be learnin' me how to rest in

you," she prayed. "Ya be a comfortin' me and I be grateful fo' that." After Clark had finished praying Marty spoke. "Be it about time to plant the garden?"

"Some of the seeds should go in now. I be thinkin' this mornin' thet I best put the plow to work on the turnin' of the ground. Should be ready fer ya in short order. Ya wantin' to plant it today?"

"Oh, yes," Marty answered with enthusiasm. "Me, I'm right eager to get a goin' on it. Only—"

"Only what?"

Marty flushed.

"Well—I never planted afore."

"Planted what?"

"Well—planted anythin'."

"Didn't yer folks have 'em a garden?"

"My ma said 'twas a nuisance, thet she'd as leave buy off a neighbor or from the store. She didn't care none fer the soil, I reckon."

"An' you?"

"I think thet I'd love to git into makin' somethin' grow. I can hardly wait to try. Only—"

Clark looked across at her evenly.

"Only?"

"Well," Marty gulped, "I know thet the garden be a woman's work, but I was wonderin'," she hesitated, "jest this one time, could ya show me how to plant the seeds an' all?"

Clark smiled to himself. He really should have volunteered rather than making her ask for his help, but it was the first time that Marty had ever asked him for anything and he took pleasure in it. He hid his smile and answered slowly, "I reckon I could—this once."

Marty looked at him, relief showing on her face. "The best time be right after dinner while the young 'uns be havin' their nap. Will the ground be plowed an' ready by then?"

Clark nodded and got up for the coffee pot to pour them a second cup of coffee. Marty nearly choked on her bite of pancake. It was the first time that she had missed getting his second cup of coffee for some months. Clark seemed unperturbed as he pushed back his plate and sat sipping slowly. When he had finished the steaming cup he left the table, reaching for his hat. "Thet be good coffee," he said, and was gone.

After the dinner dishes were done and the children were put down for their nap, Clark and Marty spread their garden seeds out on the kitchen table to decide what was to be put in at first planting and what left until later. Clark patiently showed her the different seeds, telling her what they were and the peculiarity of their growing habits. Marty listened wide-eyed. He knew so much, Clark did, and as he talked about the seeds, they took on personalities right before her eyes—like children, needing special care and attention.

Together they gathered up the seeds that were to be planted and headed for the garden. The warm sun beat down and the ground sent up a delightful warmth to meet it.

Marty reached down and let a handful of the soil trickle through her fingers. It's beautiful, she wanted to say, but it seemed such a foolish word to use to describe dirt. She had scarcely taken two steps when she realized that the temptation was too great, and turning her back to Clark, she slipped off her shoes. Then, hoisting her skirt, she peeled off her stockings. She tucked them carefully into the toes and stood barefoot, feeling the luxury of the warm earth as she dug her toes deeply into its richness. She felt like a child again—young and free, with the burdens of adulthood stripped away for the moment.

No wonder the horses like to lie down and roll when their harness is removed, she thought. Me, I'd love to be a doin' the same thing.

Clark had already busied himself preparing rows for her to place the seeds in. She went down on her knees and began to drop the tiny bits of potential life into the fertile ground.

"Someday soon, I will watch ya grow," she spoke silently to them.

Clark returned to cover the row after she had placed the seed.

"He looks to be enjoyin' it most as much as I am," thought Marty. "Oh, I wisht thet I could jest run an' skip like the calf in yonder pen. It's good jest to be a livin' on sech a day."

They worked on together, for the most part in silence, feeling a comradeship with the earth and with one another. They were nearing the end of the early planting, perhaps with some reluctance, when Clark squatted down to carefully pat earth over the sweet corn that Marty had just dropped into the ground.

Seeing his rather precarious position, Marty gave him a playful shove that sent him sprawling in the loose dirt in a rather undignified position. The look of surprise on his face was quickly displaced by one of amusement.

"Me thinks there someone be askin' fer sweet-corn kernels down her neck," he said, getting up and reaching for a handful of corn as he did so.

Marty was off on the run, but even though she was a good runner, Clark's long strides soon overtook her.

Both strong arms went about her, halting her in her escape. She writhed and twisted against him, seeking to loose herself. The laughter bubbling up within her made her fighting ineffectual. Clark tried to pin her close so that he might free his hand that held the corn kernels, but he, too, was laughing, hampering his efforts. Like two teasing children they struggled. Marty was conscious of his nearness in a way that she had never been before. The strength of the arms that held her, the beating of the heart against her cheek, the clean smell of shaving soap that still clung to him—everything about this man that held her sent funny little warm tingles through her veins. Her breath was beginning to come in little gasps; she felt powerless to struggle anymore.

The one strong arm pinned her securely against him and the free hand dumped its load of cold corn kernels down the front of her dress. Marty looked up into laughing eyes bent over her, uncomfortably close to her own. The breath caught in her throat as a strange emotion swept through her. Flight seemed to be the only answer but it must be quick, her warning signals flashed. The look on Clark's face was somehow changing from teasing to—

Marty pulled herself up abruptly.

"Thet be Clare?" she asked, putting her hands to Clark's chest and pushing with all of the strength that she could gather.

Clark let her go and she half ran, half stumbled to the house, her cheeks aflame.

Inside, in its coolness, she leaned her head against the bedroom door, trying to sort out the reason for her throbbing heart and troubled spirit. She could find no answer, and after giving herself several minutes to get herself in hand, she picked up her courage and returned to the garden, but Clark was just putting away the tools. The job was done.

Chapter 30

Sorrow

Another two weeks passed by. The green things were growing in the garden. Marty looked out of the window each morning to check on their progress. It thrilled her to watch them grow.

On the surface, things seemed to be running as normal, but deep down Marty knew that something had changed. There seemed to be an electrical charge in the air. She felt herself overly cautious lest something unexpected and unplanned should happen. Still, it was fairly easy to pretend that it wasn't there at all, and to go through the motions of the day in the same orderly fashion that she had learned to follow.

She rose early, fed Clare, got Clark's breakfast and dressed Missie. Then they had scripture reading, prayer and breakfast. She could sit across from Clark, could talk to him and share the plans for the day in as casual a way as ever, but something was different. She longed for things to stay as they had been and at the same time feared that they might.

In an effort to get herself out of her pondering, Marty wandered out to the garden to see the growing things. Somehow the garden always gave her a lift and got her thoughts off herself. She talked to the corn, pushed a little dirt around a potato plant, coaxed the onions and lettuce to hurry a bit and wondered why she had bothered with so many beans, then walked on to the fruit trees.

She was admiring each new leaf in turn when her unbeliev-
ing eyes noted that one of the trees bore blossoms. Her heart
leaped within her. Apples. Imagine, apples! Oh, if she could
only show Clark, but he was in the fields planting. Then to her
amazement she saw him coming toward her in long strides.

"Clark," she called in her eagerness. "Clark, come see."

He came to her and with her eyes fixed on the tree she
reached for his hand to draw him closer.

"Look, Clark," she almost babbled. "Apple blossoms. We
gonna have apples. Jest look."

There was no answer. She had been so sure that he would
share her excitement that she looked up in bewilderment at
the silence. Clark stood looking down at her, and in his face
she could read sorrow. Her own face went white, and her lips
quivered.

"What—what be wrong?"

He reached for her then, placing a hand on each of her
shoulders and looked deeply at her as though willing her some
of his strength to help her bear what he had to say.

"It's Laura. They done found her in the crik over by the
Conners' cabin."

"Is she—is she—?"

"She be dead."

"An' Ma?"

"She be needin' ya."

And then she was sobbing, her face against his chest. His
hands smoothed her hair as he held her close. She cried for
Ma, for Laura, for Ben, even for Sally Anne.

"Oh, God," she prayed. "Ya be the only one to be a helpin'
at a time like this. Help us all now. Please God, help us now."

Laura's body was carried to the Grahams. Marty was there
when it arrived. She would never forget the heartrending
scene that she witnessed. Ma gathered the lifeless body into
her arms, sobbing as though her heart would break, saying
over and over, "My poor baby, my poor little darlin'." Then,
after letting her grief drain from her, she wiped her tears,
squared her shoulders determinedly and began tenderly to

prepare the body for burial. Ben's grief matched Ma's, but he being a man did not feel the freedom in expressing it. Marty had never seen such an ashen face. She feared even more for Ben than for Ma.

Ben insisted on riding over to the Conners' cabin. Unknown to him, Clark had already been there. He had found a very drunk Milt who swore that he knew nothing of Laura's death. He may have roughed her up a bit, he admitted, but she was quite alive when he had last seen her, he insisted. Clark had convinced Milt that he would be wise to move farther west.

Clark rode over with Ben, making no mention of his previous visit. The cabin seemed to have been deserted for good and in a great hurry. Clark was relieved that Milt had already gone, fearing what Ben might have done in his present state of mind, and later been sorry for.

Neighbors came, and neighbors set to work. The coffin was built and the grave dug, and the frail body of the girl was committed to the ground. In the absence of a preacher, Clark was asked to say the "buryin' " words. Marty could sense just how difficult it was for him.

Solemnly they all turned from the new mound, leaving Ma and Ben to sort out and adjust to their grief. It would take time, but Ma had said that time was the answer.

Chapter 31

New Strength to Go On

June arrived bringing with her more growing things. The second cow had calved and to their great surprise, bore twin heifer calves—a special gift from God, Clark called them. The other sow had her pigs, not an exceptional litter but an acceptable one, eight, and she had kept them all.

The hatching of chicks had occurred and three proud mothers strutted about with a total of twenty-seven chicks rushing about them.

It was still too soon for Marty to have shaken off the sorrow of the tragic death of Laura. It seemed to hang about her, choking out the happiness that she wanted to feel.

Missie had had the measles and even though she was not too sick, Marty hovered over her, fearing lest another tragedy strike. But none had. It was while Missie was red-blotched and feverish that the news came that the spring's first wagon train was passing through town, heading east. There would be others. Marty's mind was filled with nursing the sick child. Missie was soon well again and her same bustling, talkative self. Even so, on this warm June day Marty still felt shackled by something; and after tucking the two youngsters in for their afternoon sleep, she decided to get out for a breath of fresh air.

She walked again through the garden, noticing how much things had grown in the days of Missie's illness. The blossoms on the apple tree had lost their petals to make room for the forming of the fruit.

She walked on past the buildings and down to the stream. She seemed drawn to that quiet spot that she had discovered long ago when she had needed comfort—then because of her own loss and now because of Ma's.

She really needed a place to think, to sort things out. Life was so confusing—the good so mixed up with the bad; such a strange combination of happiness and sorrow.

She stood leaning back against a tree trunk, watching the clear gurgling water flow.

"God," she questioned inwardly, "what be it all 'bout? I don't understand much 'bout ya. I know thet yer good. I know thet ya love'd me 'nough to die for me; but I don't understand all 'bout losin' an' hurtin'. I don't understand at all."

She closed her eyes, letting the strength of the sturdy tree trunk uphold her, listening to the rustling of the leaves, feeling the slight breeze ruffling her hair.

There was a strength there in the woods. She closed her eyes more tightly, drawing from it. When she opened them, Clark was there, sitting against a tree, his eyes on her face.

It startled her at first and she jerked upright.

"Sorry to be a frightin' ya," he told her, but then went on. "I see'd ya a comin' over here an' I thought me you'd maybe not mind me a comin' too."

"Course not."

Silence ruled for several moments. Clark picked up a small branch and broke off small pieces that he watched the stream carry away.

"Guess life be somethin' like thet stream," he said.

"Meanin'?"

"Things happen. Leaves stomp it up—animals waller in it—spring floods fill it with mud." He hesitated. "Bright sunshine makes it like a mirror glass, sparklin' rain makes it grow, but it still moves on—unchangin' like—the same stream even with the changes. It breaks through the leaves, it clears itself of the animal wallerin'—the muddy waters turn clean agin. The sunshine an' the rain it accepts, fer they give life an' strengthnen' it like, but it really could 'ave done without 'em. They're extrys like.

"Life's like thet—bad things come but life keeps on a flowin', clearing its path gradual like, easin' its own burden. The good times come; we maybe could make do without 'em, but He knows thet we need 'em to give meanin'—to strengthen us, to help us reflect the sunshine.

"Guess one has to expect the good an' the bad, long as we be a livin', an' try one's best to make the bad hurt as little as possible, an' the good—one has to help it grow like, make all the good count."

Marty had shut her eyes again as Clark began to speak. She stood there now, eyes closed, breathing deeply of the smell of the woods and the stream.

Life was like that stream. It went on. She was ready to go on now, too. She had drawn strength from the woods. No, no, that was wrong. She had drawn her strength from the God who'd made the woods.

Chapter 32

Love Comes Softly

Marty worked hurriedly on her mending. She wanted to have it all finished before she had to get supper ready. She was working on a pair of Clark's overalls, the last item in her mending basket. She was reminded again as she handled the garment, of what a big man she was married to.

"Why, they'd swaller me," she laughed, as she held them up.

Missie bustled about trying to copy her mama in what she did, as Marty had given her a scrap of cloth and a button. She threaded a blunt needle for her and showed the small child the art of button sewing.

"Ya may as well learn how it be done," she said. "Ya'll need to be a knowin' afore we know it."

Missie busied herself pushing the needle in and out of the material. Marty laughed at the child's efforts, the thread showing up in some very strange places, but Missie was quite happy with her newly learned skill.

Baby Clare lay on a rug, cooing and talking to himself and anyone else who would care to listen. He was four months old now, a bright, healthy child, who as yet had not fulfilled Clark's prediction of "wait until." All three of the members of his household doted on him, so why shouldn't he be content. Missie talked to him as she worked.

"See, baby. See big si'ter. She sewin'. Do ya like it? Look, Mama. He smiles. Clare like it—my sewin'."

Marty smiled too and went on sewing the overall patch. A loud crash made her jump and Missie exclaimed, "Dad-burn!"

"Missie, ya mustn't say thet."

"You did."

"Well, I don't anymore an' I don't want ya a' sayin' it either. Now git ya down an' pick up all of them buttons thet ya spilled."

Missie obeyed, putting the buttons in the button box and placing the box on the sewing machine.

Marty finished her patch and hurried to get supper ready. Clark would shortly be in from chores and she planned to use the supper hour to discuss moving the children's beds to the new bedroom so that she might have a bit of room to move around in her own bedroom. The rooms were finished now. She had curtains for the windows and rugs for the floors. Clark had moved his things into the one new bedroom just as soon as he was able to get a roof over it and the floor in. The other room was intended for the children.

Clare slept through the night now, and with the warmer weather Marty needn't worry about the children becoming uncovered. She felt that the time had come when she could move them out of her room without feeling anxious about them. It would be so nice to be able to reach her things without barking her shins on a small bed.

She moved hurriedly, getting the meal on when Missie came flying through the door.

"Mama—Mama—Clare sick!"

"Whatcha meanin'?" Marty stopped short.

The child grabbed her hand, jerking her toward the sitting room.

"He sick!" she screamed.

Marty ran in, hearing as she ran a rasping, gurgling sound.

She picked up the baby who was struggling furiously, his little fists flailing the air as he fought for breath.

"He's chokin'!" Marty cried as she turned him upside

down and smacked him on the back, between his tiny shoulder blades.

Clare still struggled.

"Run fer yer pa," Marty told the small child and Missie ran.

Marty reversed the baby and carefully pushed a finger down his throat. She thought that she could feel something, but the end of her finger just ticked it. Clare gagged but nothing came up.

Clark came running through the door, his eyes wild with concern.

"He's chokin'!" said Marty.

"Slap his back."

"I did." Marty was in tears now.

"Put yer finger—"

"I tried."

"I'll git the doc."

"There ain't time."

"Wrap 'im up," Clark flung at her. "I'll git the horses."

The baby was still breathing, struggling, gasping little breaths, but he was still breathing.

"Oh, God," Marty prayed. "Please help us. Please help us. Jest keep 'im breathin' 'til we reach the doc."

She grabbed a blanket and wrapped it about Clare. Missie stood, eyes wide, too frightened to even cry.

"Missie, git yer coat on," Marty ordered, "an' bring a blanket from yer bed so thet ya can lay down in the wagon."

The child hurried to obey.

Clark raced the team toward the house. Marty ran forward with the baby in her arms and Missie by the hand. Without speaking, Clark hauled Missie up, putting her and her blanket in a safe place on the wagon floor, then he helped Marty and the baby over the wheel and they were off.

The long trip to town was a nightmare. The ragged breathing of the baby was broken only by his fits of coughing. The horses plunged on, harness creaking, sweat flecking their necks and haunches. Clark urged them on and on. Marty clung to Clare, the wagon jostled her bones as though they would break, the sweat from the horses dotted her arms and face.

"We'll never make it; we'll never make it," Marty cried inwardly, as Clare's gasping little breath seemed to be weakening, and the horses' speed seemed to slacken. On they galloped, seeming to draw on a reserve that Marty would have never guessed them to have.

The baby's breathing was even more erratic as the light from the town finally came into view. Clark spoke again to the horses and they went forward with increased speed. Marty marvelled. How could they continue on at this pace? They must be ready to fall in the harness, but Clark's coaxing voice seemed to strengthen them.

Straight to the doctor's they galloped, and Clark pulled the heaving horses to a stop and jumped down before the wagon had stopped rolling. He reached up for little Clare and Marty surrendered him, and watched Clark head for the doctor's house on the run. Marty turned to help Missie up from the floor of the wagon. For a moment Marty clung to the little girl, wanting to assure her that all would be well—but would it? She climbed over the wheel and held up her arms for the child.

By the time they had entered the room that served as the doctor's office, the baby had been placed on a small table under, what seemed to Marty, a very bright light. The doctor was bending over him, appearing to completely dominate the small gasping figure as he examined him.

"He has a tiny object stuck in his throat," he said, just as though the whole world did not revolve around that very fact.

"I'm going to have to go after it. We'll have to put him to sleep. Call my Missus, will you? She helps with this—has special training."

Clark rapped loudly on the door separating the office from the living quarters and the doctor's wife came into the room. On seeing the small baby fighting for every breath, her eyes showed instant concern.

"Oh, my! What's his problem?"

"He has something in his throat. We're going to have to put him to sleep and remove it."

The doctor was already in action as he spoke, and she quickly joined him, the two working as a well-matched team.

The doctor seemed to have forgotten them for a minute as he hurriedly prepared himself; then he looked up suddenly.

"You folks can just take a chair in our living room. This won't take long, but we work best alone."

They understood and Clark took Marty's arm and led her from the room. She went reluctantly, hating to leave the fighting baby, fearing that every breath might be the last.

Clark eased her numb body into a chair. She was still clinging to Missie. He suggested that Missie could sit on another chair beside her but she shook her head. Clark himself did not sit down. Instead he paced the floor with an anxious face. Marty knew that he was petitioning his God. His hand trembled as he lifted it to remove the hat that he had forgotten. Watching him, Marty realized just how much he loved the wee baby. He loves him as though he were his own, she thought, and didn't find this strange at all. After all, she loved Missie in the same way and had as good as forgotten that there was ever a time when the little girl had been only a tiny stranger.

The centuries seemed to drag by, but in reality it was only a matter of a few minutes until the doctor appeared at the door. Clark crossed to Marty, placing a hand on her shoulder as if to protect her from hearing what they did not want to hear, but the doctor beamed at them.

"Well, Mr. Davis," he said looking at Clark, who was after all the one responsible for his coming to this town. "Your boy is going to be just fine. Had this button lodged in his throat; luckily it was turned sideways or—"

"It weren't luck," Clark responded.

"Call it what you may," the doctor went on; "it's out now. You can see him if you wish."

Marty stood up. It was then that it hit her. He was all right.

"Oh, God, he's all right. Thank Ya. Thank Ya."

If it hadn't been for Clark's arms about her, she would have gone down in a heap. He pulled her to him and they wept in thankfulness together.

Little Clare was breathing softly, no more gasping, no more fighting for each breath. Clark and Marty stood looking down at the relaxed but still white face, relief flooding through them. Marty had not released Clark's hand and his arm still steadied her.

"He's been through a lot, poor little fellow," the doctor said with feeling, and Marty felt that she'd love him forever.

"He needs a long, restful sleep now. He is still under the effect of the sleeping draught that we gave him. I expect he'll sleep through most of the night without stirring. My wife and I will take turns sitting with him. You folks had best try to get some rest. I'm sure the hotel across the street will have a room."

"Shouldn't we stay with 'im?" Marty finally found her voice.

"No need, Ma'am," the doctor answered. "He'll sleep, and seems to me that you could be using some yourself."

"He's right," Clark said. "Ya be a needin' some rest—an' some supper, too. Come on. Let's get across to the hotel."

With a last look at the sleeping baby to assure herself that he was really all right, Marty allowed herself to be led out. Clark picked up the tired and hungry Missie and carried her across the street.

Marty was glad to sink into the chair and hold Missie close, crooning words of love to her, while Clark made arrangements at the desk.

Clark returned to her.

"They'll hustle up some supper an' then show ya to a room."

Marty's eyes widened.

"What 'bout you?"

"I want to care fer the horses. They need a good rubdown an' a bit of special care."

Marty nodded. Right now she dearly loved old Dan and Charlie.

"We'll wait fer ya," she said firmly.

"Be no need—" Clark started.

"We want to."

Clark nodded and went out. While he was gone Marty told Missie what a brave girl she had been, and how she had helped baby Clare by calling her mama and getting her pa, and lying still on the wagon floor and not crying at the doctor's. She was a big girl and her mama loved her very much.

To Marty's bewilderment, large tears filled Missie's eyes and sobs shook her.

At Marty's prompting, she finally spilled forth.

"But—I spill—buttons."

Marty pulled her close, rocking her gently.

"Missie, Missie, it weren't yer fault that baby Clare found a button thet got missed a pickin' up. It jest happened, thet's all. Don't ya be a frettin' about it. Mama an' yer pa love ya so very much, an' you was a brave girl to be so good. You hush ya now."

She finally got the little girl comforted.

Clark returned, reporting that Dan and Charlie would be fine after a good rest, and they'd get it too, he declared; they'd earned it.

The three went in together to get something to eat. No one felt much like eating. Missie was too tired, Marty too spent and Clark too relieved to be much interested in food.

After making an effort to eat the food before them, they requested that they be shown to their room.

A small cot had been placed in one corner and the first thing that Marty did was to prepare Missie for bed as best she could. There was no soft warm nightie, but Missie didn't mind. She fell asleep almost before she finished her short prayer.

Marty sat beside her until she was sure that the child was asleep, then kissed her lightly again and went over to the weary Clark who was trying to relax in a large chair.

What could she say to this man who sat before her. This man who comforted her when she sorrowed, understood her joys, gave her strength when her own strength was spent, shared with her his God. There was so much that she felt. That strange, deep stirring within her—she understood it now. It was a longing for this man, his love. She wanted him, she knew that now, but how, how could she tell him?

She stood there mute, wanting to say it all, but no words came, and then he rose and reached for his hat.

"Where ya be a headin'?" She found her voice then.

"I'm a thinkin' thet I'll spend me the night over at the doc's. Iffen little Clare be a wakin' I'm thinkin' thet he should wake to some of his'n stead of strangers."

"But doc says he won't wake till morn."

"Maybe so. All the same, I'll find comfort jest watchin' him sleep peaceful-like. I'll be over in the mornin' to be sure ya not be a needin' anythin'."

He turned to go, but she knew that she mustn't let him. If he went now without knowing—

Still her voice would not obey her command. She reached out and took his sleeve. He turned to her. She could only look at him, imploring him to read in her eyes what she could not say with her lips.

He looked down at her searchingly; then he stepped closer and his hands went to her shoulders, drawing her toward him.

He must have read there what she wanted him to see, but still he hesitated a moment.

"Ya bein' sure?" he asked softly.

She nodded her head dumbly, looking deep into his eyes, and then she was in his arms, being held the way that she ached to be held, feeling the strength of his body tight against her, raising trembling lips to his.

How long had she wanted this? She wasn't sure. She only knew that it seemed forever. She loved him so much. She must later find the words to tell him so, but for now she would content herself with being held close, hearing his words of love whispered tenderly against her hair.

How did it all come about—this miracle of love? She didn't know. It had come upon her unawares—softly.